ETHEL MORTON AND THE CHRISTMAS SHIP

BY

MABELL S. C. SMITH

ETHEL MORTON AND THE CHRISTMAS SHIP

CHAPTER I

THE UNITED SERVICE CLUB AT HOME

"IT'S up to Roger Morton to admit that there's real, true romance in the world after all," decided Margaret Hancock as she sat on the Mortons' porch one afternoon a few days after school had opened in the September following the summer when the Mortons and Hancocks had met for the first time at Chautauqua. James and Margaret had trolleyed over to see Roger and Helen from Glen Point, about three quarters of an hour's ride from Rosemont where the Mortons lived.

"Roger's ready to admit it," confessed that young man. "When you have an aunt drop right down on your door mat, so to speak, after your family has been hunting her for twenty years, and when you find that you've been knowing her daughter, your own cousin, pretty well for two months it does make the regular go-to-school life that you and I used to lead look quite prosy."

"How did she happen to lose touch so completely with her family?"

"I told you how Grandfather Morton, her father, opposed her marrying Uncle Leonard Smith because he was a musician. Well, she did marry him, and when they got into straits she was too proud to tell her father about it."

"I suppose Grandfather would have said, 'I told you so,'" suggested Helen.

"And I believe it takes more courage than it's worth to face a person who's given to saying that," concluded James.

"Aunt Louise evidently thought it wasn't worth while or else she didn't have the courage and so she drifted away. Her mother was dead and she had no sisters and Father and Uncle Richard probably didn't write very often."

"She thought nobody at home loved her, I suppose," said Helen. "Father and Uncle Richard did love her tremendously, but they were just young fellows at the time and they didn't realize what their not writing meant to her."

"Once in a while they heard of Uncle Leonard through the music papers," went on Roger, "but after his health failed, Aunt Louise told us the other day, he couldn't make concert appearances and of course a man merely playing in an orchestra isn't big enough to command public attention."

"By the time that Grandfather Morton died about twelve years ago she was completely lost to the family," Helen continued, "and she says she didn't know of his death until five years after, when she came accidentally upon some mention of it in a local paper that she picked up somewhere."

"That was after Uncle Leonard's death, but it seemed to her that she could not make herself known to her people without being disloyal to his memory," Roger carried on the story.

"She probably thought that your father and uncle were just as much opposed to him as her father had been," guessed Margaret.

"As a matter of fact, they have been hunting hard for her through every clue that promised any result ever since Grandfather died because they wanted to give her her share of his property."

"He didn't cut her off with a shilling, then?"

"Grandfather seems to have had a change of heart, for he left her more than he did his sons. He said she needed it more."

"And it has been accumulating all this time."

"Seven years. That means a very pleasant increase for her and Dorothy."

"She must think rather sadly of the days when they suffered real privation for the lack of it," said Helen.

"Anyway, here they are now, with money in their pockets and an affectionate family all ready made for them and they are going to live here in Rosemont near us, and Dorothy is going to school with the Ethels, and I'm willing to admit that it comes nearer to being a romance than anything I ever heard of in real life," and Roger nodded his head gleefully.

"I'm glad she's going to live here so we can see her once in a while," said Margaret. "Mother and Sister and I all loved her at Chautauqua, she was so patient and gentle with the people she taught. And of course we all think Dorothy is a darling."

"The Ethels are crazy over her. They treat her as if she were some new belonging and they can hardly bear to have her out of their sight."

"It was Grandfather Emerson who said all summer that she looked like the Ethels," remarked Roger. "Her hair is fuzzy and her nose is puggy, but I didn't see much other likeness."

"When she grows as fat as the Ethels I think she'll look astonishingly like them. She's thin and pale, now, poor little dud."

"I wish she could grow as plump as Della Watkins."

"I saw Tom Watkins yesterday," said James.

"What was a haughty New Yorker doing on the Jersey side of the Hudson?"

"It seems he boards Cupid and his family at the Rosemont Kennels—you know they're half way between here and Glen Point. He was going to call on them."

"Dear Cupid!" laughed Margaret, recalling the bulldog's alarming face which ill agreed with his mild name and general behavior. "Let's go over to the Kennels and see him some day."

"His wife is named Psyche," went on James, "and they have two pups named Amor and Amorette."

"I should think Cupid's puppy would be the funniest little animal on earth," roared Roger. "Never, never shall I forget the day old Cupe ran away with his market wagon," and he kicked his legs with enthusiasm.

"Did Tom say anything about coming to see us?" asked Margaret.

"He said he and Della were coming over on Saturday afternoon and he inquired how far it was from Glen Point to Rosemont and whether they could make two calls in one afternoon."

"Not if he stays at either place as long as we'd like to have him," said Roger.

"Why don't we have a meeting of the United Service Club on Saturday afternoon?" suggested Helen, "and then the Watkinses can come here and you two can come and we can all see each other and at the same time decide on what we are going to do this winter."

"Great head!" approved Roger. "Can you people be here?"

"We can," assented Margaret.

"And we will." James completed the sentence for her.

"Here are the children. They've been asking when we were to have the first meeting, so I know they'll be glad to give Saturday afternoon to it."

"The children" of Helen's patronizing expression came rushing into the yard at the moment. Ethel Brown Morton, tall and rosy, her cheeks flushed with running, led the way; her cousin, Ethel Blue Morton, not quite so tall or quite so rosy, made a fair second, and their newly-found cousin, Dorothy Smith, brought up the rear, panting a trifle harder than the rest, but already looking plumper and sturdier than she had during the summer at Chautauqua.

They greeted Margaret and James gladly, and sat down on the steps of the porch to engage in the conversation.

"Hullo," a voice came through the screen door. "I'm coming out."

"That must be my friend Dicky," declared James. "Come on, old man," and he arranged his knees in position to serve as a seat for the six-year-old who calmly sat himself down upon them.

"How are you?" questioned James gravely. "All right?"

"Firtht rate," replied Dicky briefly. "Have a thuck?" and he offered James the moist end of an all-day-sucker, withdrawing it from his own mouth for the purpose.

"Thank you, I'm not eating candy to-day, sir," responded James seriously. "Much obliged to you, all the same."

Dicky nodded his recognition of James's thanks and resumed his occupation.

"It keeps us still though we're not pretty to look at as we do it," commented Ethel Brown.

"You're talking about me," asserted Dicky suddenly, once more removing his sucker from his increasingly sticky lips and fixing an accusing eye upon his sister.

"She was, Dicky, that's true," interposed Helen quickly, "but she loves you just as much as if she were talking about Roger."

Dicky regarded this as a compliment and subsided against James's chest.

"We're going to try and get the Watkinses to come out next Saturday afternoon and the Hancocks will come over and we'll have a meeting of the United Service," explained Roger to the new arrivals.

"Good enough!" approved Ethel Brown.

"What are you going to do, Madam President?" inquired Ethel Blue, who felt a lively interest in any future plans because the Club was her idea.

"We'll all think of things between now and Saturday, and suggest them then."

"Tell the Watkinses when you write to them, Helen."

"I'm just boiling over with ideas for the Club to put into execution some time or other," announced Roger.

"Big ones or little?" asked Dorothy.

"Some of them are pretty big, but I have a feeling in my bones that they'll go through."

"Good for old Roger's bones!" commended James. "May we venture to ask what some of them are?"

"'Nothing venture, nothing have,'" quoted Roger. "I'm merely saying now, however, that the biggest scheme is one that I told Grandfather Emerson about the other day and he said he'd help by giving us the house for it."

"What should we do that would need a house?"

"What do you mean—house?"

Roger grinned delightedly at the commotion he had caused.

"This plan I have is so big that we'll have to get the grown-ups to help us, but we'll do most of the carrying out ourselves in spite of that."

"I should think we would have to have their help if your plan calls for a house."

"You needn't be sarcastic, young woman. This is a perfectly good scheme— Grandfather said so. He said it was so good that he was willing to back it and to help us by supplying the house we should need."

"Poor old Roger—gone clean crazy," sighed James.

"I almost think so," agreed Helen.

"Let me tell you something, you scoffers——"

"Tell on; that's what we're waiting for."

"Well, on the whole, I guess I won't tell you a thing about it."

"If you aren't the very meanest boy I ever knew in my life," decided Margaret whole-heartedly. "To work our curiosity all up this way and then not to tell us a thing."

"I didn't get the encouragement that the plan deserved."

"Like all great inventors," commented James.

"They all come out on top at the end, I notice," retorted Roger. "You just watch me about next April when the buds begin to swell."

"Heads begin to swell at any time of year, apparently."

"Especially bad cases begin in the autumn—about September."

"Oh, you wait, just wait," threatened Roger. "When you haven't an idea what to do to make the Club really useful for another minute then you'll recall that I promised you a really big plan. Then—"

"If you aren't going to tell us now I think we'd better talk about something that has some connection with what we're going to do in September instead of this April Fool thing of yours," said Helen somewhat sharply.

"Let's not talk about it until Saturday," begged Ethel Blue. "Then we can all put our minds on it."

"I rise to remark, Madam President," continued James, "that I believe this Club has a great future before it if it does not get involved in wildcat schemes—"

"Now listen to that!" exclaimed Roger. "There speaks the canny Scot that was James's great-grandfather. Cautious old Hancock! Now you really have got me riled. I vow to you, fellow-clubmen and -women that I won't be the first to propose this scheme again. You'll have to come to me. And I'll prophesy that you will come to me about the first of next April."

"Why April?"

"Nothing to do with April Fool, I assure you. But about that time we shall have worked off all the ideas that we've cooked up to carry us through the winter and we'll be glad to undertake a service that is a service—the real thing."

"We're going to do the real thing all the time." Ethel Blue defended her idea. "But I dare say we'll want to do your thing, too."

"Grandfather's recommendation doesn't seem to count with you young know-it-alls."

"Grandfather's recommendation is the only reason why our remarks weren't more severe," retorted Ethel Brown.

"Each of us must bring in a list next Saturday," said Helen, as they all walked to the corner to see that the Hancocks took the car safely.

"And I believe that every one will be a perfectly good plan," said Roger magnanimously.

"There won't be one that will require a house to hold it anyway," retorted Margaret.

CHAPTER II

DOROTHY'S COTTAGE

ROSEMONT and Glen Point were two New Jersey towns near enough to New York to permit business men to commute every day and far enough away from the big city to furnish plenty of air and space for the growing generation. It was the latter qualification that endeared them to the Morton and Hancock families, for there were no commuters in their households. Lieutenant Morton, father of Roger and Helen and Ethel Brown and Dicky, was on his ship in the harbor of Vera Cruz. Captain Morton, his brother, father of Ethel Blue, had returned to Gen. Funston's army after finding their sister, Mrs. Smith, at Chautauqua and convoying her with all the Mortons and Mrs. Morton's father and mother, Mr. and Mrs. Emerson, back to Rosemont. His short furlough did not allow him to remain long enough to see his sister established in a house of her own, but it was understood that she was to hire a furnished house as near as possible to the Mortons' and live in it until she made up her mind where she wanted to build.

"Dorothy and I have wandered about the United States so long," she said plaintively, "that we are thankful to settle down in a town and a house that we can call our own, and we shall be even happier when we have a bungalow actually belonging to us."

At present they were still staying with the Mortons, but the Morton family was so large that two visitors crowded them uncomfortably and Mrs. Smith felt that she must not trespass upon her sister-in-law's hospitality longer than was absolutely necessary.

"I think the white cottage just around the corner will be the one that we will take," she said to Dorothy. "Come with me there again this afternoon for one more look at it, and then we'll make up our minds."

So they went to the white cottage and carefully studied its merits.

"The principal good thing about it is that it is near Aunt Marion's," declared Dorothy.

"I think so, too. And it is near school and church and the butcher's and baker's and candlestick-maker's. We shan't have very far to walk for anything."

"Oh, Mother, it doesn't seem possible that this can be us really living and not just perching around, and having enough money and enough to eat and nothing to worry about."

Mrs. Smith threw her arm about Dorothy's shoulder.

"The thing for you to do to show your gratitude is to grow well and strong just as fast as you can. I want to see you as rosy as the Ethels."

"They run me around so much that I think they'll do it for me before very long."

"They have a start, though, so you'll have to do all the vigorous things that they do and others too."

"You mean exercises at home?"

"Every morning when you get up you should do what a cat does when he wakes from a nap."

"I know—he stretches himself way out to the tips of his claws."

"And shakes himself all over. What do you suppose he's doing it for?"

"To stretch his muscles, I should think."

"And to loosen his skin and make himself generally flexible. Have you ever seen a sick cat? His coat looks dull and dry and woolly instead of silky, and when you feel of him his skin doesn't slip over his bones easily. It wouldn't be very complimentary to ourselves to say that you and I are sick cats just now, but it wouldn't be far from the truth."

"I don't much like the sound of it," laughed Dorothy. "What can we invalid pussies do to get well?"

"A few simple exercises we ought to take every morning when we first get out of bed. We ought to stand first on one foot and then on the other, and swing vigorously the foot that is off the floor."

"That's easy."

"Then if we stretch our arms upward as high as we can, first one and then the other and then both, and then put our hands on the ribs of each side and stretch and lift them we shall have limbered up the lower and the upper parts of ourselves pretty thoroughly."

"I learned a good exercise for the waist muscles at the Girls' Club last summer. You sit down and roll the body at the waist line in all directions. You can do it standing, too; that brings in some different muscles."

"We'll do that. These few exercises will wake up every part of the body."

"We ought to do them with the windows open."

"When you first wake up after having the windows wide open all night you don't realize the cold in your room. It isn't until you have been to a warmer room that you notice the cold in your bedroom. So the best time to take these exercises is just the minute you hop out of bed. Stand in front of the open window and take deep breaths of air way down into the very lower tips of your lungs so that every tiny cell will be puffed out with good, fresh oxygen."

"It will take a lot of time to do all those exercises."

"Five minutes every morning will be enough if we do them vigorously. And you mustn't forget that your aim is to catch up with the Ethels."

"And then to beat them. I'll do it."

They went slowly through the cottage and planned the purpose to which they would put each room. It was simply furnished, but all the necessities were there.

"It's more fun this way than if there were a lot of furniture," said Dorothy, "because we can get what is lacking to suit ourselves."

"All the time that we are here we can be making plans for building our own little house."

"I can hardly wait to have it."

They hugged each other in their happiness and the tears were not far from the eyelids of both of them, for Mrs. Smith had not known anything but the actual necessities of living for many years and Dorothy had never known many comforts that had been every day matters and not luxuries to her mother's youth.

So Mrs. Smith hired the white cottage and she and Dorothy moved in at once. A cousin of Mary, Mrs. Morton's old servant, who had been Dicky's nurse, came to work for them, and by the time of the first meeting of the United Service Club Dorothy felt so settled in her new home that she wanted to have the meeting in the living-room or the big attic just to see how it felt to be entertaining people in her own house.

"I think I wouldn't suggest it this time," Mrs. Smith warned her. "Helen is the president, you see, and it seems more suitable for the first meeting to be held at her house. Ask if you mayn't have the next one here. How often are you going to meet?"

"I hope it will be once a week, and so does Ethel Blue. She thinks there's plenty of occupation to keep a service club busy all the time."

At noon the sun disappeared and the Rosemont members of the U. S. C. began to have doubts as to whether the Hancocks and Watkinses would appear.

"Even if it rains hard I think James and Margaret will come," said Helen. "The trolley brings them almost from their door to ours; but I don't feel so sure about the Watkinses."

"It doesn't take but ten minutes longer for them to come out from New York than for the Hancocks to come over from Glen Point."

"But they have to cross the ferry and take the train and it seems more of an undertaking than just to hop into a street car."

"It's getting so dark and gloomy—what do you say if you Ethels make some candy to enliven the afternoon?"

"Is there time before they come?"

"Just about. Try Vinegar Candy this time. If you leave half of it unstirred and stir the other half it will be as good as two kinds, you know."

So the Ethels went off into a pantry back of the kitchen, where Mrs. Morton had had a small gas stove installed so that the children might cook to their hearts' content without interfering with the occupants of the kitchen.

"There's nothing that upsets people who are trying to make a house run smoothly and to do its work promptly and well as to have children come into the kitchen and use the stove when it is needed for other purposes, and get in the way and leave their cooking apparatus around and their pots and pans uncleaned," declared Mrs. Morton.

So the Ethels and Helen, and Roger, too, for he was a capital cook and was in great demand whenever the boys went on camping trips, all contributed from their allowances to buy a simple equipment for this tiny kitchen which they called their own. Mrs. Morton paid for the stove, but the saucepans and baking tins, the flour and sugar and eggs, the flavoring extracts and the seasonings were all supplied by the children, and it was understood that when a cooking fit seized them they must think out beforehand what they were going to want and provide themselves with it and not call on the cook or Mary to help them out of an emergency caused by their own thoughtlessness. Mrs. Morton was sure that her reputation as a sensible mother who did not let the children over-run the kitchen at times when they were decidedly in the way was one of the chief reasons why her servants stayed with her so long.

So now Ethel Brown said to Ethel Blue, "Have we got all the materials we need for Vinegar Candy?" and Ethel Blue seized the cook book and read the receipt.

"Mix together three cupfuls of sugar, half a cupful of vinegar, half a cupful of water. When it comes to a boil stir in one teaspoonful of soda."

"We've got sugar and soda and water," announced Ethel Brown after investigating the shelves of the tiny storeroom, "but there isn't any vinegar. I do hate to go out in this rain," for the dark sky was making good its threat.

"I'll get it for you. Give me your jug," said Roger, swinging into his raincoat. "I'll be back in half a jiff," and he dashed off into the downpour, shaking his head like a Newfoundland dog, and spattering the drops as he ran.

He was back before the Ethels had their pans buttered and the water and sugar measured, so briskly had he galloped. It was only a few minutes more before the candy stiffened when a little was dropped into a cup of cold water.

"Now we'll pour half of it into one of the pans," directed Ethel Brown, "and then we'll get Roger to beat the other half so it will be creamy."

Roger was entirely willing to lend his muscles to so good a cause and soon had the mass grained and white.

"Good work; one boiling for two batches!" he declared. "That pleases my notions of scientific management."

When the door-bell rang for the first arrivals the whole thing was almost cold, and Mary, who was always willing to help in an emergency, hastened the chilling process by popping the tins into the ice box.

"They're not warm enough any longer to melt the ice," she decided, "so I'll just hurry 'em up a bit."

After all the discussion about the city dwellers' dislike of going into the suburbs it was the Watkinses who came first.

"We're ahead of the hour," apologized Della. "We couldn't time ourselves exactly for so long a distance."

"The Hancocks will come just on the dot, I've no doubt," laughed Tom. "Old James is just that accurate person!"

As the clock's hand was on the appointed minute a whir at the bell announced Margaret and James, both dripping from their run from the corner.

"Mrs. Morton's compliments and she thought they had better drink this so they won't get cold."

"Our compliments and thanks to Mrs. Morton," returned Tom, his hand dramatically placed over a portion of his person which is said to be the gateway to a boy's heart.

When the cups had been emptied and the wafers consumed and the Ethels had taken away the tray with the remains of the feast and had brought back the two kinds of candy, carefully cut into squares and heaped in two of the pretty Japanese bowls which made a part of their private kitchen equipment, they all settled down in big chairs and on couches except Roger, who sat near the fire to stir it, and Helen, who established herself at one end of the table where she could see them all conveniently.

CHAPTER III

THE CHRISTMAS SHIP

"THE meeting will come to order," commanded Helen, her face bubbling with the conflict between her dignity and her desire to laugh at her dignity.

"We haven't any secretary, so there can't be any minutes of the last meeting."

Helen glanced sidewise at James, for she was talking about something she never had had occasion to mention in all her life before and she wondered if he were being properly impressed with the ease with which she spoke of the non-existent minutes.

James responded to her look with an expression of surprise so comical that Helen almost burst into laughter most unsuitable for the presiding officer of so distinguished a gathering.

"Oughtn't we to have a secretary?" asked Tom. "If we're going to have a really shipshape club this winter it seems to me we ought to have some record of what we do."

"And there may be letters to write," urged Roger, "and who'd do them?"

"Not old Roger, I'll bet!" cried James in humorous scorn.

"I don't notice that anybody is addressing the chair," remarked Helen sternly, and James flushed, for he had been the president's instructor in parliamentary law at the meeting when the Club was organized, and he did not relish being caught in a mistake.

"Excuse me, Madam President," he apologized.

"I don't see any especial need for a secretary, Miss President," said Margaret, "but can't we tell better when we're a little farther along and know what we're going to do?"

"Perhaps so," agreed Helen. "There isn't any treasurer's report for the same reason that there isn't any secretary's," she continued.

"Just to cut off another discussion I'd like to repeat my remark," said Margaret.

"If we become multi-millionaires later on we can appoint a treasurer then," said Della, her round face unusually grave.

"Instead of a secretary's report it seems to me it would be interesting to remember what the Club did last summer to live up to its name," suggested Tom. "You know Della and I weren't elected until after you'd been going some time, and I'm not sure that I know everything that happened."

The Mortons and Dorothy and the Hancocks looked around at each other rather vaguely, and no one seemed in a hurry to begin.

"It looks to me as if a secretary is almost a necessity," grinned Tom, "if nobody remembers anything you did!"

"There were lots of little things that don't seem to count when you look back on them," began Ethel Blue.

"We did some things as a Club," said Roger, "and we can tell Watkins about those without embarrassing anybody."

"Our first effort was on Old First Night," said Margaret thoughtfully. "Don't you remember we went outside the gate and picked flowers and decorated the stage?"

"In the evening James and Roger passed the baskets to collect the offering in the Amphitheatre," Ethel Blue said. "And then we all did things that helped along in the Pageant and on Recognition Day."

"I don't think those really counted for much as service," said Helen, "because they were all of them mighty good fun."

"I think we ought to do whatever will help somebody, whether we like it or not," declared Ethel Blue, "but I don't see why we shouldn't hunt up pleasant things to do."

"What are we going to do, anyway?" asked Della. "Has anybody any ideas? Oh, please excuse me, Helen—Miss President—perhaps it wasn't time to ask that question."

"I was just about to ask for suggestions," said Helen with dignity. "Has any one come across anything that we can do here in Rosemont or in Glen Point or in New York? Anything that will be an appropriate beginning for the United Service Club? We want to do something that would be suitable for the children of our father and uncle who are serving in the Army and Navy trying to keep peace in Mexico, and of a man like Doctor Hancock, who is serving his fellowmen in the slums every day, and of a clergyman who is helping people to do right all the time."

Helen flushed over this long speech.

"Rosemont, Glen Point, and New York—a wide field," said Tom dryly. "It seems as if we might find something without much trouble."

"I thought of the orphanage in Glen Point," said Margaret.

"What is there for us to do for the kids there that the grown people don't do?" asked Roger.

"The grown people contribute clothes and food and all the necessaries, but sometimes when I've been there it seemed as if the children didn't have much of any of the little nothings that boys and girls in their own homes have. It seemed to me that perhaps we could make a lot of things that weren't especially useful but were just pretty; things that we'd like to have ourselves."

"I know just how they feel, I believe," said Margaret. "One of my aunts thinks that perfectly plain clothes are all that are necessary and she won't let my cousins have any ruffles or bows. It makes them just miserable. They're crazy for something that 'isn't useful.'"

"How would it do to get together a lot of things for Christmas for the orphans? We might offer to trim a tree for them. Or to give each one of them a foolish present or a pretty one to offset the solid things the grown-ups will give."

"When I was a kid," observed James, "I used to consider it a mean fraud if I had clothing worked off on me as Christmas presents. My parents had to clothe me anyway; why should they put those necessities among my Christmas gifts which were supposed to be extras!"

"There you are again; what people want in this world of pain and woe, ye-ho, he-ho," chanted Roger, "is the things they can go without."

"Has any one thought of anybody else we can benefit?" questioned Helen. "We might as well have all the recommendations we can."

"There's an old couple down by the bridge on South Street," said Roger. "I've often noticed them. They're all bent up and about a thousand years old. We might keep an eye on them."

"I know about them," contributed Ethel Brown. "I asked about them. They have a son who takes care of them. He gives them money every week, so they aren't suffering, but they both have the rheumatism frightfully so they can't go out much and I shouldn't wonder if they'd like a party some time, right in their own house. If we could go there and sing them some songs and

Dicky could speak his piece about the cat and we could do some shadow pantomimes on a sheet and then have a spread, I believe they'd have as good a time as if they'd been to the movies."

"We'll do it." Tom slapped his leg. "I'll sing 'em a solo myself."

Groans rose from James and Roger.

"Poor old things! What have you got against them?"

"Oh, well, if you're jealous of my voice—of course I wouldn't for the world arouse any hard feelings, Madam President. I withdraw my offer. But mark ye, callow youths," he went on dramatically, "the day will come when I'm a Caruso and you'll be sorry to have to remember that you did your best to discourage a genius that would not be discouraged!"

"The meeting will come to order." Helen rapped for quiet, for the entire room was rocking to and fro over Tom's praise of one of the hoarsest voices ever given to boy or man.

"We'll give the old people a good show, even if Tom does back out," cried Roger. "I wish we had a secretary to put down these suggestions. I'm afraid we'll forget them."

"So am I," agreed Helen. "Let's vote for a secretary. Roger, pass around some paper and pencils and let's ballot."

Roger did as he was bid, and Ethel Brown and Della collected the ballots and acted as tellers.

"The tellers will declare the vote," announced Helen, who had been conferring with James while the balloting was going on, and had learned the proper parliamentary move. Margaret had coached Ethel Brown so that she made her report in proper style.

"Total number of votes cast, eight; necessary to a choice, five. Margaret has one, Dorothy has one, Roger has two, Ethel Brown has one, Ethel Blue has three. Nobody has enough."

"Have we got to vote over again?" Helen asked of James.

"I move you, Madam President, that we consider the person receiving the highest number of votes as the person elected and that we make the election unanimous."

"Is the motion seconded?"

Cries of "Yes," "I second it," "So do I," came from all over the room and included a call from Ethel Blue. Roger pealed with laughter.

"Ethel Blue means to get there," he shouted.

"I do? What have I done?" demanded Ethel Blue, so embarrassed at this attack that the tears stood in her eyes.

"Why, you're the person who's receiving a unanimous election," returned Roger, between gasps. "You've made it unanimous, yourself, all right."

Poor Ethel Blue leaned back in her chair without saying a word.

"Roger, you're too mean," cried Helen. "Don't you mind a word he says, Ethel Blue. It's very hard to follow votes and it isn't at all surprising that you didn't understand."

"What does it mean?"

"It means that you're elected secretary."

"But there weren't enough votes."

"You had three and Roger had two, and nobody else had more than one. When one candidate has more than the rest he may be considered as elected, even if he didn't get the right number of votes—that is, if everybody agrees to it."

"And you agreed to it," chuckled Roger.

"Stop, Roger. You're our new secretary, Ethel Blue, and it's very suitable that you should be, for the club was your idea and you ought to be an officer. Roger, give Ethel Blue your pencil and the rest of that paper you had for the ballots. Come and sit next to me, Ethel."

Ethel Blue felt that honors were being thrust upon her much against her will, but she was afraid that she would make some other mistake if she objected, so she meekly took the pencil and paper from Roger and began to note down the proceedings.

"We've had a suggestion from Glen Point and one from Rosemont—let's hear from New York," said the president. "Della—anything to say?"

"Papa can suggest lots of people that we can help if we ask him," said Della. "I didn't ask him because I thought that perhaps you'd have some pet charities out here where there aren't so many helping hands as there are in New York."

"How about you, Tom?"

"To tell you the truth," responded Tom gravely, "I didn't think up anything to suggest this afternoon because my mind has been so full of the war that I can't seem able to think about anything else."

Everybody grew serious at once. The war seemed very close to the Mortons, although it was a war across the sea, because they knew what it would mean to their father and uncle if ever our country should be involved in war. The thought of their own mental suffering and their anxiety if Captain and Lieutenant Morton should ever be sent to the front had given them a keen interest in what had been going on in Europe for six weeks.

"I read the newspapers all the time," went on Tom, "and I dare say I don't gain much real information from them, but at least I'm having ground into my soul every day the hideous suffering that all this fighting is bringing upon the women and children. The men may die, but at least they can fight for their lives. The women and children have to sit down and wait for death or destruction to come their way."

"It's too big a situation for us way off here to grasp," said Roger slowly, "but there are people on the spot who are trying to give assistance, and if Americans could only get in touch with them it seems as if help might be handed along the way we handed the water buckets last summer when the cottage was on fire."

"The Red Cross is working in all the countries that are at war," said Helen. "There's an American Red Cross and people are sending clothing and food to the New York branch and they are sending them on to Europe. That's Roger's bucket brigade idea."

"Why don't we work for the Red Cross?" asked Della.

"I saw in the paper a plan that seems better still for us youngsters," said Ethel Blue. "Some people are going to send over a Christmas ship with thousands and thousands of presents for the orphans and the other children all over Europe. Why don't we work for that? For the Santa Claus Ship?"

"'Charity begins at home,'" demurred Margaret.

"We needn't forget the Glen Point orphans. The Christmas Ship is going to sail early in November and we'll have plenty of time after she gets off to carry out those other schemes that we've spoken of."

"I'd like to move," said Ethel Brown, getting on to her feet to make her action more impressive, "that the United Service Club devote itself first to preparing a bundle to send off on the Christmas Ship. After that's done we can see what comes next."

"Does any one second the motion, that we work first for the Christmas Ship?" asked Helen.

Every voice in the room cried "I do."

"All in favor?" There was a chorus of "Ayes."

"Contrary minded?" Not a sound arose.

"It's a unanimous vote that we start right in on the bundle for the Santa Claus Ship."

CHAPTER IV

FINANCIAL PLANS

"This parliamentary business fusses me," exclaimed Helen. "Let's just talk, now that we've decided what we are going to do."

"Take a more comfortable chair," suggested Tom, pulling over a Morris chair nearer the fire.

Roger stirred up the flames and tossed on some pine cones.

"These cones remind me that our old people down by the bridge might like some. They have a funny open stove that they could use them in."

"What are they good for? Kindling?" asked Della.

"Ha! There speaks the city lady used only to steam! Certainly they are good for kindling on account of the pitch that's in them, but they're also great in an open fire to brighten it up when it is sinking somewhat and one or two at a time tossed on to a clear fire make a pretty sight."

"And a pretty snapping sound," added Dorothy, remembering the cones from the long leaf pines.

"Our old couple gets a bushel on Monday afternoon if it ever stops raining," promised Roger. "Dicky loves to pick them up, so he'll help."

"The honorary member of the United Service Club does his share of service work right nobly," declared James, who was a great friend of Dicky's.

"The thing for us to do first is to decide how we are to begin," said Helen.

"We might talk over the kinds of presents that the war orphans would like and then see which of them any of us can make," suggested Margaret wisely.

"Any sort of clothing would come in mighty handy, I should think," guessed James, "and I don't believe the orphans would have my early prejudices against receiving it for Christmas gifts."

"Poor little creatures, I rather suspect Santa Claus will be doing his heaviest work with clothing this year."

"As far as clothing is concerned," said Margaret, "we needn't put a limit on the amount we send or the sizes or the kinds. The distributors will be able to use everything they can lay their hands on when the Christmas Ship comes in and for many months later."

"Then let's inquire of our mothers what there is stowed away that we can have and let's look over our own things and weed out all we can that would be at all suitable and that our mothers will let us give away, and report here at the next meeting."

"While we're talking about the next meeting," broke in Dorothy while the others were nodding their assent to Helen's proposition, "won't you please come to my house next time?"

"We certainly will," agreed Della and Margaret.

"You bet," came from the boys.

"And Mother told me to offer the Club the use of our attic to store our stuff in. It's a big place with almost nothing in it."

"I'm sure Aunt Marion will be glad not to have anything else go into her attic," said Ethel Blue, and all the Mortons laughed as they thought of the condition of the Morton attic, whose walls were almost bulging with its contents.

"If that's settled we must remember to address all our bundles to 'Mrs. Leonard Smith, Church Street, Rosemont,'" James reminded them.

"It seems to me," Ethel Brown said slowly, thinking as she spoke, "that we might collect more clothing than we shall be able to find in our own families."

"There are a good many of us," suggested Della.

"There are two Watkinses and two Hancocks and five Mortons and one Smith—that's ten, but if the rest of you are like the Morton family—we wear our clothes pretty nearly down to the bone."

All the Mortons pealed at this and the rest could not help joining in.

"One thing we must not do," declared Helen. "We must not send a single old thing that isn't in perfect order. It's a poor present that you have to sit down and mend."

"We certainly won't," agreed Margaret. "I wear my clothes almost down to the skeleton, too, but I know I have some duds that I can make over into dresses for small children. I'm gladder every day that we took that sewing course last summer, Helen."

"Me, too. My dresses—or what's left of them—usually adorn Ethel Brown's graceful frame, but perhaps Mother will let us have for the orphans the clothes that would ordinarily go to Ethel Brown."

Ethel Brown looked worried.

"Ethel Brown doesn't know whether that will mean that she'll have to go without or whether she'll have new clothes instead of the hand-me-downs," laughed Roger.

"I don't care," cried Ethel Brown. "I'd just as lief go without new clothes if Mother will let the Club have the money they'd cost."

"I've been thinking," said Tom, "that we're going to need money to work this undertaking through successfully. How are we going to get it?"

"But shall we need any to speak of?" inquired Margaret. "Fixing up our old clothes won't cost more than we can meet ourselves out of our allowances. I'm going to ask my Aunt Susy to let me have some of the girls' old things. The girls will be delighted; they're the ones who have the plain clothes."

"We'll fix them up with ruffles and bows before we send them away," smiled Helen.

"Why can't we ask everybody we come across for old clothes?" Ethel Blue wondered.

"Grandmother Emerson would be sure to have something in her attic and I shouldn't wonder if she'd be willing to ask the ladies at the Guild if they'd contribute," said Helen.

"Do we want to take things from outside of the Club?" objected Ethel Brown.

"I don't see why not," answered Margaret. "The idea is to get together for the orphans as many presents as possible, no matter where they come from. We're serving the orphans if we work as collectors just as much as if we made the clothes ourselves."

"Right-o," agreed Roger. "Let's tackle everybody we can on the old clo' question. We can ask the societies in our churches—"

"Why not in all the churches in town?" dared Ethel Blue.

The idea brought a pause, for the place was small enough for the churches to meet each other with an occasional rub.

"I believe that's a good idea," declared Tom, and as a clergyman's son they listened to his views with respect. "All the churches ought to be willing to come together on the neutral ground of this club and if we are willing to take the responsibility of doing the gathering and the packing and the expressing to the Christmas Ship I believe they'll be glad to do just the rummaging in their attics and the mending up."

"We needn't limit their offerings to clothes, either," said Della. "We'll take care of anything they'll send in."

"Let's put it up to them, I say," cried Roger. "There's at least one member of the Morton family in every society in our church and we ought to get the subject before every one of those groups of people by the end of next week and start things booming."

"We'll do the same at Glen Point," agreed Margaret.

"I can't promise quite as much for New York, because I don't know what Father's plans are for war relief work in his church, but I do feel pretty sure he'll suggest some way of helping us," said Della.

"That's decided, then—we'll lay our paws on everything we can get from every source," Tom summed up the discussion. "Now I come back to what I said a few minutes ago—I think we're going to need more money to run this association than we're going to be able to rake up out of our own allowances, unless Margaret's is a good deal bigger than mine," and he nodded toward Margaret, who had objected to the more-money idea when he had offered it before.

"Just tell me how we'll need more," insisted Margaret.

"I figure it out that the part we boys will have to do in this transaction will be to district this town and Glen Point and make a house to house appeal for clothes and any sort of thing that would do for a Christmas present, all to be sent to Mrs. Smith's."

"That won't cost anything but a few carfares, and you can stand those," insisted Margaret.

"Carfares are all right and even a few express charges for some people who for some reason aren't able to deliver their parcels at Mrs. Smith's house. But if you girls are going to make over some of these clothes and perhaps make new garments you'll need some cash to buy materials with."

"Perhaps some of the dry goods people will contribute the materials."

"Maybe they will. But you mark my words—the cost of a little here and a little there mounts up amazingly in work of this sort and I know we're going to need cash."

"Tom's right," confirmed Della. "He's helped Father enough to know."

The idea of needing money, which they did not have, was depressing to the club members who sat around the fire staring into it gloomily.

"The question is, how to get it," went on Tom.

"People might give us money just as well as cloth, I suppose," suggested Margaret.

"I think it would be a thousand times more fun to make the money ourselves," said Ethel Blue.

"The infant's right," cried Tom. "It will be more fun and what's more important still, nobody can boss us because he's given us a five dollar bill."

"I suppose somebody might try," murmured Helen.

"They would," cried Tom and Della in concert.

"We aren't a clergyman's children for nothing," Tom went on humorously. "The importance a five dollar bill can have in the eyes of the giver and the way it swells in size as it leaves his hands is something that few people realize who haven't seen it happen."

"Let's be independent," cried Dorothy decidedly, and her wish was evidently to the mind of all the rest, for murmurs of approval went around the room.

"But if we're so high and mighty as not to take money contributions and if we nevertheless need money, what in the mischief are we going to do about it?" inquired Roger.

"We must earn it," said Helen. "I'll contribute the money Mother is going to pay me for making a dozen middy blouses for the Ethels. She ordered them from me last summer when I began to take the sewing course and I haven't quite finished them yet, but I'll have the last one done this week if I can get home from school promptly for a day or two."

"I can make some baskets for the Woman's Exchange," said Dorothy.

"I learned how to make Lady Baltimore cake the other day," said Margaret, "and I'll go to some ladies in Glen Point who are going to have teas soon and ask them for orders."

"I can make cookies," murmured Ethel Brown, "but I don't know who'd buy them."

"You tell the kids at school that you've gone into the cooky business and you'll have all the work you can do for a while," prophesied Roger. "I know your cookies; they're bully."

"I don't notice that we boys are mentioning any means of making money," remarked James dryly. "I confess I'm stumped."

"I know what you can do," suggested Margaret. "Father said this morning that he was going to get a chauffeur next week if he could find one that wouldn't rob him of all the money he made. You can run the car—why don't you offer to work half time—afternoons after school, for half pay? That would help Father and he'd rather have you than a strange man."

"He'd rather have half time, too. He likes to run the car himself, only he gets tired running it all day on heavy days. Great head, Sis," and James made a gesture of stroking his sister's locks, to which she responded by making a face.

"I know what I can do," said Roger. "You know those bachelor girls about seventy-five apiece, over on Church Street near Aunt Louise's—the Miss Clarks? Well, they had an awful time last year getting their furnace attended to regularly. They had one man who proved to be a—er," Roger hesitated.

"Not a total abstainer?" inquired James elegantly.

"Thank you, Brother Hancock, for the use of your vocabulary. The next one stole the washing off the line, and the next one—Oh, I don't know what he did, but the Miss Clarks were in a state of mind over the furnace and the furnace man all winter. Now, suppose I offer to take care of their furnace for them this winter? I believe they'd have me."

"I think they'd be mighty glad to get you," confirmed Helen. "Could you do that and take care of ours, too?"

"Sure thing, if I put my mind on it and don't chase off with the fellows every time I feel in the mood."

"Mother would like to have you take care of ours if you could manage three," said Dorothy.

"I'll do it," and Roger thumped his knee with decision.

"I wouldn't undertake too much," warned Helen. "It will mean a visit three times a day at each house, you know, and the last one pretty late in the evening."

"I'm game," insisted Roger. "You know I can be as steady as an old horse when I put my alleged mind on it. Mother never had any kick coming over my work in the furnace department last winter."

"She said you did it splendidly, but this means three times as much."

"I'll do it," and Roger nodded his head solemnly.

"It seems to be up to Della and me to tell what we can do," said Tom meditatively. "Father's secretary is away on a three months' holiday and I'm doing his typewriting for him and some other office stunts—as much as I can manage out of school hours. I'll turn over my pay to the Club treasury."

This was greeted with applause.

"I don't seem to have any accomplishments," sighed Della, her round head on one side. "The only thing I can think of is that I heard the ladies who have charge of the re-furnishing of the Rest Room in the Parish House say that they were going to find some one to stencil the window curtains. I might see if they'd let me do it and pay me. I didn't take that class at the Girls' Club last summer, but Dorothy and Ethel Brown could teach me."

"Of course."

"Or you could get the order from them, I'd fill it, and you could make the baskets for the Woman's Exchange," offered Dorothy.

Della brightened. That was a better arrangement.

"Try it," nodded Tom. "If you turn out one order well you'll get more; see if you don't."

"Our honorary member, Mr. Dicky Morton, might sell newspapers since he got broken in to that business last summer," laughed Ethel Brown. "Mother wouldn't let him do it here, I know, but he can weave awfully pretty things that he learned at the kindergarten and if there are any bazars this fall he could sell some of them on commission."

"Dicky really understands about the Club. I think he'd like to do something for the orphans," Helen agreed.

"Ladies and gentlemen," announced Ethel Blue, rising in her excitement; "I have a perfectly grand, galoptious idea. Why do we wait for somebody else to get up a bazar to sell Dicky's weaving? Let's have a bazar of our own. Why can't we have a fair with some tables, and ice cream and cake for sale and an entertainment of some kind in the evening? We all know all sorts of stunts; we can do the whole thing ourselves. If we announce that we are doing it for the Christmas Ship I believe everybody in town would come—"

"—And in Glen Point and New York," Roger mocked her enthusiasm.

"You know we could fill the School Hall as easy as fiddle, Roger. You see everybody would know what we were at work on because we are going to begin collecting the clothes right off, so everybody will be interested."

Tom nodded approval.

"Perhaps we can do the advertising act when we do the collecting."

"If I drive Father, I see myself ringing up all the neighboring houses while he's in on his case," said James, "and it's just as easy to talk bazar part of the time as it is to chat old clo' the whole time."

"Can you get the School Hall free?" asked Tom.

"We'd have to pay for the lighting and the janitor, but that wouldn't be much," said Roger. "It would be better than the Parish House of any of the churches because if we had it in a church there'd surely be some people who wouldn't go because it was in a building belonging to a denomination they didn't approve of, but no one can make any kick about the schoolhouse."

"It's the natural neighborhood centre."

"We'll have the whole town there."

"If we let in some of the school kids we'll get all their families on the string," recommended Roger.

"I'm working up a feat that I've never seen any one do," said Tom. "I'll turn it loose for the first time at our show."

"Remember, you're all coming to me next Saturday afternoon," Dorothy reminded them as the Hancocks and Watkinses put on their overgarments and sought out their umbrellas preparatory to going home.

"And we'll bring a list of what we can contribute ourselves and what we've collected so far and what we think we can collect and we'll turn in anything we've made."

"If there's anything we can work on while the Club is going on we'd better bring it," suggested Helen.

"Mother says we may have the sewing machine in the attic," said Dorothy.

"I believe I'll take my jig-saw over," suggested Roger. "Aunt Louise wouldn't mind, would she?"

"She'd be delighted. Bring everything," and Dorothy glowed with the hospitality that had been bottled up in her for years and until now had had but small opportunity to escape.

CHAPTER V

ROGER GOES FORAGING

ALTHOUGH Helen never had been president of any club before, yet she had seen enough of a number of associations in the high school and the church to understand the advantage of striking while the iron of enthusiasm was hot. For that reason she and Roger worked out the districting of Rosemont before they went to bed that night, and the next afternoon Roger went over to Glen Point on his bicycle, and, with James's help, did the same for that town. It was understood that Tom would not be able to come out again until Saturday, but he had agreed to be on hand early in the morning to do a good half day of canvassing. The girls were to speak to every one to whom they could bring up the subject conveniently, wherever they met them.

Roger began his work on Monday afternoon after school. He wheeled over to a part of the town where he did not know many people, his idea being that since that would be the most disagreeable place to tackle he would do it first and get it over with. He was a merry boy, with a pleasant way of speaking that won him friends at once, and he was not bothered with shyness, but he did hesitate for an instant at his first house. It was large and he thought that the owner ought to be prosperous enough to have plenty of old clothes lying about crying to be sent to the war orphans.

It was a maid whose grasp on the English language was a trifle uncertain who opened the door. Roger stated his desire.

"Old clothes?" she repeated after him. "I've no old clothes to give you," and she shut the door hastily.

Roger stood still with astonishment as if he were fastened to the upper step. Then his feelings stirred.

"The idiot!" he gasped. "She thought I wanted them for myself," and he looked down at his suit with a sudden realization that his long ride over one dusty road and a spill on another that had recently been oiled had not improved the appearance of his attire. However, he rang the bell again vigorously. The woman seemed somewhat disconcerted when she saw him still before her.

"I don't want the clothes—" began Roger.

"What did you say you did for?" inquired the maid sharply, and again she slammed the door.

By this time Roger's persistency was roused. He made up his mind that he was going to make himself understood even if he did not secure a contribution. Once more he rang the bell.

"You here!" almost screamed the girl as she saw once more his familiar face. "Why don't you go? I've nothing to give you."

"Look here," insisted Roger, his toe in the way of the door's shutting completely when she should try to slam it again; "look here, you don't understand what I want. Is your mistress at home?"

The girl was afraid to say that she was not, so she nodded.

"Tell her I want to see her."

"What's your name?"

"I'm Roger Morton, son of Lieutenant Morton. I live on Cedar Street. Can you remember that?"

She could not, but her ear had caught the military title and upstairs she conveyed the impression that at least a general was waiting at the door. When the mistress of the house appeared Roger pulled off his cap politely, and he was such a frank-faced boy that she knew at once that her maid's fears had been unnecessary, though she did not see where the military title came in. Roger explained who he was and what he wanted at sufficient length, and he was rewarded for his persistency by the promise of a bundle.

"I know your grandmother, Mrs. Emerson," said the lady, who had mentioned that she was Mrs. Warburton, "and your aunt, Mrs. Smith, has hired one of my houses, so I am glad on their account to help your enterprise, though of course its own appeal is enough."

Roger thanked her and took the precaution to inquire the names of her neighbors, before he presented himself at another door. He also reached such a pitch of friendliness that he borrowed a whisk broom from Mrs. Warburton and redeemed his clothes from the condition which had brought him into such disfavor with the maid-servant.

There was no one at home in the next house, but the next after that yielded a parcel which the old lady whom he interviewed said that he might have if he would take it away immediately.

"I might change my mind if you don't," she said. "I've been studying for ten days whether to make over that dress with black silk or dark blue velvet. If I give the dress away I shan't be worried about it any longer."

"Very well," cried Roger, and he rolled the frock up as small as he could and fastened it to his handle bars.

There was no one at home at the next house, but the woman who came to the door at the next after that listened to his story with moist eyes.

"Come in," she said. "I can give you a great many garments. In fact there are so many that perhaps I'd better send them."

"Very well," returned Roger. "Please send them to my aunt's," and he gave the address.

"You see," hesitated Roger's hostess, now frankly wiping her eyes, "I had a little daughter about ten years old, and—and I never have been willing to part with her little dresses and coats, but how could I place them better than now?"

Roger swallowed hard.

"I guess she'd like to have 'em go over there," he stammered, and he was very glad when he escaped from the house, though he told his mother, "she seemed kind of glad to talk about the kid, so I didn't mind much."

"Count listening as one of the Club services," replied Mrs. Morton.

Back in his own part of town Roger felt that his trip had been profitable. A very fair number of garments and bundles had been promised, and he had told everybody he could to watch the local paper for the announcement of the entertainment to be given by the U. S. C.

"Everybody seemed interested," he reported at home. "I don't believe we'll have a mite of trouble in getting an audience."

It was at a cottage not far from the high school that Roger came upon his nearest approach to an adventure. When he touched the buzzer the door was opened by an elderly woman who spoke with a marked German accent. Roger explained his errand. To his horror the woman burst into tears. When he made a gesture of withdrawal she stopped him.

"My son—my son is mit de army," she exclaimed brokenly. "My son und de betrothed of my daughter. We cannot go to the Fatherland. The German ships go no more. If we go on an English or French ship we are kept in England. Here must we stay—here."

"You're safe here, at any rate," responded Roger, at a loss what reply to make that would be soothing in the face of such depressing facts.

"Safe!" retorted the woman scornfully. "Who cares to be safe? A woman's place is mit her men when they are in danger. My daughter and I—we should be in Germany and we cannot get there!"

"It's surely a shame if you want to go as much as that," returned Roger gently, and just then to his surprise there came through an inner door a young woman whom he recognized as his German teacher in the high school, Fräulein Hindenburg. Her face was disfigured with weeping and he knew now why she had seemed so ill and listless in her classes.

"You must not mind Mother," she said, looking surprised as she saw one of her pupils before her. "It is true that we would go if we could but we cannot, so we must stay here and wait."

Roger explained his errand.

"To work for the war orphans of all countries?" cried both women excitedly. "Gladly! Gladly!"

"We are knitting every day—scarfs, socks, wristlets," said the older woman. "Also will we so gladly make clothing for the children and toys and playthings—what we can."

Fräulein smiled a sad assent and Roger wheeled off, realizing that the pain caused by the war no longer existed for him only in his imagination; he had seen its tears.

So freely had people responded to Roger's appeal that he began to wonder how the Club was going to take care of all the garments that would soon be coming in. After that thought came into his mind he made a point of asking the givers if they would send their offerings as far as possible in condition to be shipped.

"Margaret and Helen can make over some of the clothes and the Ethels and Dorothy can help with the simple things, I suppose, but if there are many grown-up dresses like this one on my handle bar they won't have time to do anything else but dressmake," meditated Roger as he pedalled along.

Nowhere did he meet with a rebuff. Every one was pleased to be asked. Many offered to make new garments. One old woman who lived in a wheel-chair but who could use her hands, agreed to sew if the material should be sent her. Many mothers seemed to consider it a Heaven-sent opportunity to make a clearance of the nursery toys though Roger stoutly insisted that they must all be in working order before they were turned in.

"It's been perfectly splendid," breathed Roger joyfully as he finished his third afternoon and came into the house to report to his mother and Helen. "It's a delight to ask when you feel sure that you won't have to coax as you usually do when you're getting up anything. Everybody seems to jump at the chance."

Toward the end of the week Ethel Blue came in beaming.

"I've got some entirely new people interested," she cried.

"Who? Who?"

"The last people you'd ever think of—the women in the Old Ladies' Home."

"Why should you think them the very last to be interested?" asked Mrs. Emerson who happened to be at the Mortons' and whose fingers were carrying the flying yarn that her needles were manufacturing into a sock. "Most of them are mothers and it doesn't take a mother to be interested in such a cause as this. Every human being who has any imagination must feel for the sufferings of the poor children."

"It seemed queer to me because I've never seen them do anything but just sit there with their hands in their laps."

"Poor souls, nobody ever provides them with anything to do."

"Now all of them say that they'll be delighted to sew or knit or do anything they can if the materials are provided for them."

"Here's where we can begin to spend the money Mother has offered to advance us," cried Ethel Brown. "Can't we go right after school to-morrow and buy the yarn for them, Mother?"

"Indeed you may. Has Della sent you the knitting rules from the Red Cross yet?"

"We're expecting them in every mail. If they don't come before we take the wool to the Home we can start the ladies on scarfs. They're just straight pieces."

"Mrs. Hindenburg and Fräulein are knitting wristlets for the German soldiers. They could give the rule for them, I should think," suggested Roger, "and our old lady friends can just cut it in halves for the kids."

It was the next day that Helen came in from school all excitement.

"I've made a discovery as thrilling as Roger's about Fräulein!" she cried.

"What? Who is it about? Tell us."

"It's about Mademoiselle Millerand."

"Your French teacher?" asked Mrs. Emerson.

"She was new at school last year and you've heard us say she's the most fascinating little black-eyed creature."

"Perhaps she can't talk fast!" added Roger.

"What's the story about her?" demanded Ethel Brown.

"It's not a romantic story like Fräulein's; that is, there's no betrothed on the other side that she's crazy to get to; but she's going over to join the French Red Cross."

"That little thing!" cried Roger. "Why she doesn't look as if she had strength enough to last out a week!"

"She says she's had a year's training in nursing and that a nurse is taught to conserve her strength. She hopes she'll be sent to the front."

"The plucky little creature! When is she going?"

"As soon as she can put in a substitute at the school; she doesn't want to leave us in the lurch after she made a contract for the year."

"It may take some time after that to arrange for a sailing, I suppose."

"Perhaps so. Any way I think it would be nice if we gave her a send-off—"

"Just as we will Fräulein if her chance comes."

"We can make some travelling comforts."

"She won't be able to carry much," warned Mrs. Morton.

"Everything will have to be as small as possible, but we can hunt up the smallest size of everything. I think it will be fun!"

"She'll probably be very much pleased."

"I wish there was something rather special we could do for Fräulein too, so we could be perfectly impartial."

"Watch for the chance to do something extra nice for her. She's having the harder time of the two; it's always harder to stay and wait than it is to go into action, even when the action is dangerous."

While the Mortons were canvassing Rosemont, James and Margaret were doing the same work in Glen Point. Dr. Hancock had accepted his son's offer and James was now regularly engaged as his father's chauffeur, working after school hours every school day and on Saturday mornings. The Doctor insisted that he should have Saturday afternoons free so that he might go to the Club. He was also quite willing that James should follow the plan he had sketched at the last Club meeting and visit the neighbors of his father's patients while Doctor Hancock was making his professional calls. The plan worked to a charm and James found Glen Point quite as ready as Rosemont to respond to the "bitter cry of the children."

"So many people are getting interested I almost feel as if it weren't our affair any longer," James complained to his father as they were driving home in the dusk one afternoon.

"Look out for that corner. That's a bad habit you have of shaving the curbstone. You needn't feel that way as long as your club is doing all the organizing and administration. That's the part that seems to make most people hesitate about doing good works. It isn't actual work they balk at; it's leadership."

"If handling the stuff and disposing of it is leadership then we're a 'going concern' all right," declared James. "Roger telephoned over this morning that the bundles were coming in to Mrs. Smith's at a great rate, and that a lot of people were making new garments and things that will turn up later."

"When is Tom coming out?"

"Saturday morning. I've saved one district for him to do then and that will finish up Glen Point as Roger and I sketched it out."

"It hasn't been so hard a job as you thought."

"Chasing round in the car has saved time. This is a bully job of yours, Dad."

"You won't hold it long if you cut corners like that, I warn you again."

"I'll try to cut 'em out," laughed James as he carefully turned into the Hancocks' avenue.

CHAPTER VI

IN THE SMITH ATTIC

"GRANDFATHER EMERSON wants to give the Club a present," cried Ethel Brown as the last arrivals, the Hancocks, came up the stairs and entered the attic of Dorothy's house on Saturday afternoon.

The large room was half the width of the whole cottage and, with its low windows and sloping roof had a quaint appearance that was increased by its furnishing of tables and seats made from boxes covered with gay bits of chintz. Dorothy had not neglected her work for the orphans but she had found time to fit up the meeting place of the U. S. C. so that its members might not have to gather in bare surroundings. The afternoon sun shone brightly in through simple curtains of white cheesecloth, the sewing machine awaited Helen beside a window with a clear north light, and Roger's jig-saw was in a favorable position in a corner. Each one who came up the stairs gave an "Oh" of pleasure as the door opened upon this comfortable, cheerful room where there was nothing too good to be used and nothing too bad to have entrance to the society of beauty-loving folk. "What did your grandfather give us?" asked Margaret.

"Grandfather has been awfully interested in the Club from the very beginning, you know. The other day he asked if we wouldn't like to have him give us club pins with our emblem on them."

"How perfectly dear of him!" ejaculated Delia.

"Don't let your hopes rise too high. I said it would be simply fine to have little forget-me-not pins like those we talked about at our very first meeting in the ravine at Chautauqua—do you remember?"

"Blue enamel," murmured Dorothy.

"He said he wanted us to have them, and that it was a lovely symbol and so on, and he'd seen some ducks of pins in New York that were just what we'd like, and some single flower ones for the boys—"

"Um. This suspense is wearing on me," remarked Roger.

"We talked it over and the way it came out was that Grandfather said that perhaps he'd better give us now the money the pins would cost and keep his present for later."

No one could resist a groan.

"He won't forget it. Grandfather never forgets to do what he promises. We'll get them some time or other. But I had a feeling that we'd like them later better even than now because we'd feel then that we'd really earned them after the Club had done something worth while, you know."

"I suppose we will," sighed Della, "but they do sound good to me."

"He was bound that we should have the forget-me-not in some form or other," went on Ethel Brown, "and he's sent us a rubber stamp with 'U. S. C.' on it and a forget-me-not at each end of the initials. There's an indelible pad that goes with it and we are to stamp everything we send out on some part where it won't be too conspicuous."

"It will be like signing a letter to the child the present goes to," said Dorothy.

"Isn't he a darling!" exclaimed Ethel Blue. "I love him as much as if he were my own grandfather."

"He turned the money right over into my hand," continued Ethel Brown— "the money he didn't spend for the pins, I mean. It's fifteen dollars. What shall I do with it?"

"Pay for the yarn you bought for the women in the Old Ladies' Home to knit with," said Helen promptly.

"'"The time has come," the walrus said,'" quoted Tom, "when we must have a treasurer. It was all very well talking about not needing one when we didn't have a cent of money, but now we are on the way toward being multis and we can't get on any longer without some one to look after it."

"Let's make Tom treasurer and then he can fuss over the old accounts himself," suggested Roger.

Roger's loathing for keeping accounts was so well known that every one laughed.

"Not I," objected Tom. "I'm not at all the right one. It ought to be one of you people who live out here where we're going to do our work. You'll have hurry calls for cash very often and it would be a nuisance to have to wait a day to write or phone me. No, sir, Roger's the feller for that job."

"No, Roger isn't," persisted that young man disgustedly. "I buck, I kick, I remonstrate, I protest, I refuse."

"Here, here," called Ethel Blue. "Who said you could have James's vocabulary?"

"Well, James, then," said Tom. "It doesn't make much difference who it is as long as he lives in these precincts and not as far away as I do. Madam President, I nominate Mr. Hancock for treasurer of the United Service Club."

"You hear the nomination," responded Helen. "Is it seconded?"

"I second it with both hands and an equal number of feet," replied Roger enthusiastically.

"Now is the opportunity for a discussion of the merits of the candidate," observed Helen drily.

"There are many things that might be said," rejoined Dorothy, "but because it would probably embarrass him—"

"Oh, say!" came from James. "Are they as bad as that?"

"As I was remarking when I was interrupted," continued Dorothy severely, "because it might make the candidate feel queer if he were to hear all the compliments we should pay him, I think we won't say anything."

"I'll trust old Roger not to pay compliments," responded James.

"Old Roger is in such a good humor because this job is being worked off on to your shoulders instead of his that he might utter some blandishments that would surprise you."

"I wouldn't risk it!"

"Are you ready to vote?" asked Helen.

"We are," came ringing back, and the resulting ballot placed James in the treasurership, the only dissenting vote being his own. His first official act after the money was put into his hands was to give it back to Ethel Brown in part repayment of the sum which her mother had advanced for the yarn for the Old Ladies' Home.

"Here's another bundle," announced Mrs. Smith, appearing with a large parcel as the Club members were looking over the collection that had come in. All the contributions were piled in a corner, and already they made a considerable mound.

"Roger will have to apply some of his scientific management ideas to that mass of stuff," laughed Mrs. Smith.

"I wish we could spread them out so that we could get an idea of what is which."

"Couldn't we boys make some sort of rack divided into cubes or even knock together a set of plain shelves? That would lift them off the floor."

"I wish you would," said Helen. "Then we ought to put a tag on each bundle telling who sent it and what is in it."

"And what we think can be done with it, if it isn't in condition to send off just as it is," added Ethel Brown.

"I believe I saw some planks in the cellar that would make sufficiently good shelves for what you need," said Mrs. Smith. "Suppose you boys go down stairs with me and take a look at them while the girls are making out the tags."

So the boys trooped after their hostess while Ethel Brown unscrewed the cap of her fountain pen and wrote on the tags that Dorothy cut out of cardboard, and Ethel Blue fitted them with strings, so that they might be tied on to the parcels.

"These dresses and coats came from Mrs. Ames," said Helen. "They belonged to her daughter who died, and they're all right for a child of ten, so we'll just mark the bundle, 'From Mrs. Ames,' and 'O.K.,' and put it away."

"There's an empty packing box over in that corner," said Dorothy. "Wouldn't it be a good scheme to put the bundles we shan't have to alter at all, right into it?"

"Great. Then we shan't have to touch them again until the time comes to tie them up in fancy paper to make them look Christmassy."

"Here's the dress Mrs. Lancaster couldn't decide whether to have made over with black silk or blue velvet."

"Mrs. Lancaster," murmured Ethel Brown, making out her card.

"That certainly can't go as it is," pronounced Della.

"There's material enough in it for two children's dresses," decided Margaret. "Mark it, 'Will make two dresses.'"

"Here's Maud Delano's jacket. She told Roger she'd send this over when she got her new one."

"It came this morning. It's all right except for tightening a button or two," and Ethel Brown inscribed, "Coat; tighten buttons" on the slip which Della tied on to one of the incompetent fasteners.

"Good for Mrs. Warburton!" cried Helen.

"What's she done?"

"Here's a great roll of pink flannelette—and blue, too—among her things. We can make dresses and wrappers and sacques and petticoats out of that."

"It always seems just as warm as woolen stuff to me," said Dorothy. "Of course it can't be."

"Cotton is never so warm as wool, but if it's warm enough why ask for anything different. What's in your mind?" inquired Margaret.

"I was wondering if we couldn't do something to forward the cotton crusade at the same time that we're helping the war orphans."

"You mean by making things out of cotton materials?"

"Yes. The orphans will want the warmest sort of clothing for winter, I suppose, but spring is coming after winter and summer after that, and I don't believe anything we send is going to be wasted."

"They might wear two cotton garments one over the other," suggested Della.

"I don't say that we'd better make all our clothes out of cotton material, but where it doesn't make any especial difference I don't see why we shouldn't choose cotton stuff. After all, it's the war that has spoiled the cotton trade so we're still working for war sufferers only they'll be on this side of the Atlantic. You know they say the southern cotton planters are having a serious time of it because they aren't selling any cotton to speak of in Europe."

"Let's do it!" cried Ethel Blue and she told their decision to James who had come up to measure the attic doorway for some reason connected with the planks they had found.

"It's a great idea. Bully for Dorothy," he cried working away with a footrule. "This will go all right," he decided, and ran down again to give a lift to the other carpenters.

There were eight planks each about six feet long that Mrs. Smith had discovered in the cellar. A telephone to Mrs. Warburton had gained her consent to their use and the boys set about fitting them together as soon as they were on the top floor. Fortunately they were already planed and of so good a length for the purpose they were to be used for that nothing was needed but hammer and nails to produce a set of shelves quite adequate for the purpose. Two of the boards made the sides, and between them the remaining six were nailed at intervals.

"We can set it against the wall over here," decided Tom, "and it won't need a back."

"Which is lucky," James declared, "cos there ain't no planks to make a back of."

"Let's nail a block of wood or a triangle of wood under the bottom shelf in the corners," advised Roger, "so the animal won't wobble."

"If we had enough wood and a saw we could make nice cubby-holes, one for each bundle," remarked Tom, his head on one side.

"Tom's getting enthusiastic over carpentering. We haven't either any more wood or a saw, old man, so there won't be any cubby-holes this time," decreed Roger.

"It will do perfectly well this way," said Helen. "Now if you'll help us up with these bundles—"

It was a presentable beginning for their collection. Two parcels in addition to Mrs. Ames's had gone into the packing case in the corner, but three shelves of the new set were filled with tight rolls, each with its tag forward so that no time would be lost in examining the contents, again.

"That's what I call a good beginning," announced Helen after the boys had swept up their shavings and had taken them and their hammers and the remaining nails down stairs.

"What next, Madam President?" inquired James when they returned. The girls were already spreading out the pink and blue flannelette on a plank table that had been left in the attic by the carpenters who had built the house.

"We are going to cut some little wrappers out of this material. I think you boys had better fix up some sort of table over on that side of the room and get your pasting equipment ready, for we'll need oodles of boxes of all sizes and you might as well begin right off to make them."

"Right-o," agreed Roger. "Methinks I saw an aged table top minus legs leaning against the wall in the cellar. Couldn't we anchor it on to this wall with a couple of hinges and then its two legs will be a good enough prop?"

"If they're both on the same side."

"It seems to me they are."

"Any superfluous hinges around the house, Dorothy?"

"I'm afraid not."

"Never mind, I'll get a pair when I go after the pasteboard and the flour for the paste and a bowl for a pastepot, and a—no, three brushes for us three boys to smear the paste with and some coarse cotton cloth for binders."

"Don't forget the oil of cloves to keep your paste from turning sour," Dorothy cried after them.

"And mind you boil it thoroughly," said Margaret.

The boys started again towards the cellar when Roger's eye happened to fall on the cutting operations of the girls.

"Pshaw!" he cried in scorn. "You are time-wasters! Why don't you cut out several garments at once and not have to go through all that spreading out and pinning down process every time? I saw a tailor the other day cutting a pile of trousers two feet high."

"What with, I should like to know?" inquired Della mystified.

"He did have a knife run by electricity," admitted Roger, "but there's no reason why you can't cut four or five of those things just as easily as one."

"We'll go on down and get the table top," said James, and he and Tom departed.

"Now, then, watch your Uncle Roger. Is this tissue paper affair your pattern? All you need to do is to fasten your cloth tightly down on to your table four thicknesses instead of one. Thumb tacks, Dorothy? Good child! Now lay your pattern on it—yes, thumb-tack it down if you want to—and go ahead. You've got new, sharp shears. Don't be in a hurry. There you are—and you've saved yourself the fuss of doing that three times more."

Pattern for Wrapper Pattern for Wrapper

e c e = twice the length from floor to neck

a b = slit

Fold cloth on line c b d

Sew together sides f to e

Insert sleeves c to f

"Roger really has a lot of sense at times," admitted Ethel Brown, after her brother had leaped down the attic stairs in pursuit of the boys.

"He is good about helping," added Della.

"What is this garment—a wrapper?" asked Margaret as Helen held up the soft flannelette.

Wrapper Completed Wrapper Completed

"Yes, it's the simplest ever, and we can adapt one pattern to children of all sizes or to grown people," explained Helen.

"I never heard of anything so convenient!"

"First, you measure the child from the floor to his neck—I measured this on Dicky. Then you cut a piece of material twice that length. That is, if the kiddy is thirty inches from the floor to the chin you cut your flannelette sixty inches long."

"Exactly. Then cut a lengthwise slit thirty inches long. Then fold the whole thing in halves across the width of the cloth and sew up the sides to within four and a half inches of the top and you have a wrapper all but the sleeves."

"How do you make those?"

"It takes half a yard for a grown person—a quarter of a yard for a youngster. Cut the width in halves and double it and sew it straight into the holes you've left at the tops."

"Will that be the right length?"

"You can shorten it if you like or lengthen it by a band. You finish the slit up the front by putting on a band of some different color. It looks pretty on the ends of the sleeves, too. We can use blue on this pink and pink on the blue."

"It's easy enough, isn't it? I think I'll make myself one when we get through with the Ship."

"All you need to know is the length from the person's chin to the floor and you can make it do for anybody. And all you need to do to make a short sacque is to know the length from the person's chin to his waist. I have a notion we'll have some wee bits left that we can make into cunning little jackets for babies."

"I don't see why this pattern wouldn't do for an outdoor coat if you made it of thicker cloth—eider-down, for instance."

"It would. Gather the ends of the sleeves about an inch down so as to make a ruffle, and put frogs or buttons and loops on the front and there you have it!"

"Did you bring a petticoat pattern, Margaret?" asked Ethel Blue.

"Haven't you seen the pictures of European peasant women and little girls with awfully full skirts? I believe they'd like them if we just cut two widths of the same length, hemmed them at the bottom, and ran a draw-string in the top. We can feather-stitch the top of the hem if we want to make it look pretty, or we can cut it a little longer and run one or two tucks."

"Or we might buttonhole a scallop around the edge instead of hemming it," suggested Ethel Brown.

"You know I believe in doing one thing well," said Dorothy. "How would it do if we Club girls made just coats and wrappers and sacques from that pattern of Helen's, and petticoats? We can make them of all sorts of colors and a variety of materials and we can trim them differently. We'd be making some mighty pretty ones before we got through."

"I don't see why not," agreed Margaret thoughtfully. "Let's do it."

"I brought the Red Cross knitting directions," said Delia. "I didn't get them till this morning."

"Grandmother will be delighted with those. She's going to take them to the Old Ladies' Home and start them all to work there."

"Are you sure they'll knit for the children?"

"She's going to ask them to knit for the children now, with bright-colored yarns. Afterwards they can knit for the soldiers, and then they must use dark blue or grey or khaki color—not even a stripe that will make any poor fellow conspicuous."

As they finished reading the instructions they heard the boys tramping upstairs with their paraphernalia.

"It looks to me, Dorothy," said Tom, "as if you had us on your hands for most of these club meetings, to do our work here. Are you sure Mrs. Smith doesn't mind?"

"Mother is delighted," Dorothy reassured him. "And she wants you all to come down and have some chocolate."

CHAPTER VII

FOR A TRAVELLER'S KIT

ONCE the Club was started on its work it seemed as if the days were far too short for them to accomplish half of what they wanted to do. Mrs. Morton insisted that her children should have at least two hours out of doors every day, and that cut down the afternoons into an absurdly brief working time. Mrs. Smith had electric lights installed in her attic and it became the habit of the Mortons and often of the Hancocks to meet there and cut and sew and jig-saw and paste for an hour or two every evening. The Watkinses were active in New York evidently, for Della sent frequent postcards asking for directions on one point or another and Tom exchanged jig-saw news with Roger almost daily.

Meanwhile the war was in every one's mind. The whole country realized the desirability of trying to obey President Wilson's request for neutrality in word, thought, and deed. The subject was forbidden at school where the teachers never referred to the colossal struggle that was rending Europe and the children of varied ancestries played together harmoniously in the school yard. If at the high school Fräulein and Mademoiselle were looked at with a new interest by their scholars no word suggestive of a possible lack of harmony was uttered to them, and their friendship for each other seemed to increase with every day's prolongation of the war.

In the Morton family war discussion was not forbidden and the events of the last twenty-four hours as the newspapers reported them were talked over at dinner every evening. Mrs. Morton thought that the children should not be ignorant of the most upheaving event that had stirred the world in centuries, but she did not permit any violent expressions of partisanship.

"You children are especially bound to be neutral," she insisted, "because your father and Ethel Blue's father are in the service of our country, and a neutrality as complete as possible is more desirable from them and their families than from civilians."

A new idea was blossoming in the young people's minds, however. They had grown up with the belief that armament was necessary to preserve peace. Great men and good had said so. "If we are prepared for war," they declared, "other nations will be afraid to fight us." Captain and Lieutenant Morton had agreed with them, as was natural for men of their profession. They did not believe in aggression but in being ready for defense should they be attacked.

Now it seemed to Roger and Helen as they read of the sufferings of invaded France and the distress of trampled Belgium that no country had the right to benefit by results obtained through such cruel means.

"Just suppose a shell should drop down here just as we were walking along," imagined Roger as he and Helen were on their way to school. "Suppose Patrick Shea's cornfield there was marched over before the corn was harvested and all these houses and churches and schools were blown up or burned down and all the people of this town were lying around in the streets dead or wounded!"

"When you bring it home to Rosemont it doesn't sound the way it does when you read in the histories about a 'movement' here and a 'turning of the right flank' there, and 'the end of the line crumpling up.' When the line crumples up it means fathers and brothers are killed and women and children starve—"

"Think what it would be to have nothing to eat and to have to grub around in the fields and devour roots like the peasants in the famine time in Louis XIV's reign."

"And think about the destruction of all the little homes that have been built up with so much care and happiness. Mary told me her sister bought a chair one month and a table at another time when she and her husband came across bargains," said practical Ethel Brown who had caught up with them. "They've furnished their whole house the way we children have added to our kitchen tins and plates; and then everything would be broken to smash by just one of those shells."

"The people who've been spreading the gospel of peace for years and years needn't be discouraged now, it seems to me," observed Roger thoughtfully, "even if it does look as if all their talk had been for nothing. These horrors make a bigger appeal than any amount of talk."

"Grandfather Emerson says that perhaps universal peace is going to be the result of the war. It seems far off enough now."

"It will be dearly bought peace."

"Hush, there goes Mademoiselle. I wonder when she's going to sail."

"Why don't you ask her to-day? The Club must give her some kind of send-off, you know."

"I wonder if she'd mind if we went to New York to see her start?"

"It won't be hard to find out. We can tell her that we won't be offended if she says 'No.'"

"If she's willing we might take that opportunity to go over the ship. I've always wanted to go over an ocean steamer."

"Perhaps they won't let anybody do it now on account of the war. It will be great if we can, though."

The Service Club learned more geography in the course of its studies of the war news than its members ever had learned before voluntarily. The approach of the German army upon Paris was watched every day and its advance was marked upon a large map that Roger had installed in the sitting-room. When the Germans withdrew the change of their line and its daily relation to the battle front of the Allies was noted by the watchful pencil of one or another of the newspaper readers.

Thanks to the simplicity of the pattern which the Club had adopted for its own they were enabled to make a large number of gay garments in a wonderfully short time. From several further donations of material they made wrappers for children of fourteen, twelve, ten, down to the babies, adding to each a belt of the same color as the band so that the garments might serve as dresses at a pinch. They found that with the smaller sizes they could cut off a narrow band from the width of the cloth at each side, and that served as trimming for another garment of contrasting color.

When they had constructed a goodly pile of long wrappers they fell upon the short sacques, and before many days passed a mound of pink-banded blue and blue-banded pink, and red-banded white and white-banded red rose beside their machines. Della wrote that she was using her mother's machine and was learning how better and better every day. Thanks to their lessons at Chautauqua Margaret and Helen sewed well on the machine already. Ethel Brown and Ethel Blue and Dorothy basted on the bands and the belts and added the fastenings. It was their fingers, too, that feather-stitched and cat-stitched the petticoats that came into being with another donation of flannelette. Dorothy was glad when any new material was cotton as every yard that they used helped the South to rid itself of its unsold crop.

"Ladies are going to wear cotton dresses all winter, they say," she told the Club at one of its meetings. "Mother is going to let me have all my new dresses made of cotton stuff and she's going to have some herself."

"We wear cotton middies all winter," protested the Ethels who felt as if Dorothy felt that they were not doing their share to help on the cause she was interested in.

"When Aunt Marion gets your new dancing school dresses couldn't you ask her to get cotton ones?"

"I suppose we could. Do you think they'd be pretty enough?"

"Some cotton dresses that are going to be worn on the opening night of the opera at the Metropolitan are to be on exhibition in New York in a week or two."

"If cotton is good enough for that purpose I guess it's good enough for your dancing class," laughed Helen.

"Mother says they make perfectly beautiful cottons now of exquisite colors and lovely designs. Don't you think it would be great if we set the fashion of the dancing class?"

"Let's do it. Mother says silk isn't appropriate for girls of our age, anyway."

"If you can be dressed appropriately and beautifully at the same time I don't see that you have anything to complain of," smiled Helen.

With the short time that the girls had at their command every day it did not seem as if they would be able to do much with the garments that came in to be made over. There were not many of these because the boys had been instructed after the first day to ask that alterations and mending be done at home, but there were a few dresses like Mrs. Lancaster's that were on their hands. Mrs. Smith came to their help when this work bade fair to be too much for them.

"I'll ask Aunt Marion and Mrs. Emerson and Mrs. Hancock and Mrs. Watkins to lunch with me some day," she promised Dorothy, "and after luncheon we'll have an old-fashioned bee and rip up these dresses and then we can see what material they give us and we can plan what to do with them."

The scheme worked out to a charm. The elders enjoyed themselves mightily and the resulting pile of materials, smoothly ironed and carefully sorted gave Margaret and Helen a chance to exercise their ingenuity. Mrs. Watkins took back to town with her enough stuff for two, promising to help Della with them, and the suburban girls, with the assistance of the grown-ups, made six charming frocks that looked as good as new.

It was early in October that Helen rushed home from school one day with the news that Mademoiselle was going to sail at the end of the week.

"We must begin to-day to make up a good-bye parcel for her," she cried.

"Red Cross nurses are allowed a very small kit," warned Mrs. Morton.

"We can try to make things so tiny that she won't have to leave them behind her when she goes on duty, but even if she does she can give them to somebody who can make them useful."

"I'll make steamer slippers to begin with," said Ethel Brown.

"How?" asked Ethel Blue.

Top of Slipper Top of Slipper

Sew a and b together

"You get a pair of fleecy inner soles—they have them at all the shoe stores—and then you cut a top piece of bright colored chintz just the shape of the top part of a slipper and you sew it together at the back and bind the edges all around."

"How do you put the top and the sole together?"

"The edge of the sole is soft enough to sew through. You turn the top inside out over the sole and sew the binding of the chintz on to the edge of the sole over and over and when you turn it right side out there you are with gay shoes."

"They'll fill up a bag, though," commented Ethel Blue. "I should think you might make a pair just like that only make the sole of something that would double up. Then they'd go into a case and be more compact."

"That's a good idea, too," agreed Ethel Brown. "What could you use for a sole?"

"Soft leather would be best. I imagine you could get a piece from the cobbler down town. Or you could get the very thin leather that they used at Chautauqua for cardcases and pocket books—the kind Roger uses—and stitch two pieces together."

"Why wouldn't a heavy duck sole do?" suggested Mrs. Emerson.

"If you stepped on a pin it wouldn't keep it out as well as leather," objected her daughter.

"I believe I'll try a pair with a flowery chintz top and a duck sole covered with chintz like a lining to the shoe," said Ethel Blue slowly as she thought it out. "Then I'll make the case of two pieces of chintz bound together."

"One piece ought to be longer than the other so that it would be a flap to come over like an envelope."

This was Ethel Brown's contribution to the slipper building.

"You could fasten it with a glove snapper. I got some the other day for my leather work," said Roger. "I'll put them on for you."

"Why don't you Ethels make both kinds?" suggested Dorothy. "She'll find a use for them."

"If you girls will make it I'll contribute the silk for a bath wrap that she can throw over her warm one, just for looks, on the boat," said Mrs. Emerson. "I have one I use on sleeping cars and it rolls up into the smallest space you can imagine."

Slipper Case Slipper Case

Place section a on section b and sew edges together, leaving c d open

e = Snap fastening

"Good for Grandmother!" cried a chorus of voices.

"Can we use our famous wrapper pattern?" asked Helen.

"I don't see why not. Mine has a hood but that isn't a difficult addition if you merely shape the neck of your kimono a little and then cut a square of the material, sew it across one end and round the lower end a trifle to fit into the neck hole you've made."

"How about longer sleeves, Mother?" asked Mrs. Morton.

"I think I would make them longer. And I'd also make an envelope bag of the same silk to carry it in on the return trip from the bath. You'll be surprised to find into how small an envelope it will go."

"Put a cord from one corner of the envelope to the other so that Mademoiselle may have her hands free for her soap and towel and other needfuls," advised Mrs. Smith, who had been listening to the suggestions.

"Wouldn't another envelope arrangement of chintz lined with rubber cloth make a good washrag bag or sponge bag?" asked Ethel Brown.

"Nothing better unless you put a rubber-lined pocket in a Pullman apron."

This hint from Grandmother Emerson aroused the curiosity of the young people.

"What is a Pullman apron? Tell us about it," they cried.

"Mine is made of linen crash," said Mrs. Emerson. "Dorothy will insist on your making yours of cotton chintz and it will be just as good and even prettier. Get a yard. Cut off a piece thirty inches long and make it fourteen wide. Bind the lower edge with tape. Turn up six inches across the bottom and stitch the one big pocket it makes into smaller ones of different sizes by rows of up and down stitching. Make a bag of rubber cloth just the right size to fit one of the larger pockets. Take the six inches that you cut off from your yard of material and bind it on both edges with tape. Stitch that across your apron about four inches above the top of the lower row of pockets. Divide the strip into as many pockets as you want to for hairpins and pins and neck arrangements, and so on."

"Your apron has two raw edges now," said Helen.

"Bind it on each side with tape. That will finish it and it will also fasten the edges of the pockets securely to the apron. Sew across the top a tape long enough to serve as strings."

Pullman Apron Pullman Apron

d b plus the turned up portion, b a, = inches

b a = inches

b b = inches

c c c = pockets

d d = strings

"The idea is to roll all your toilet belongings up together in your bag, eh?"

"Yes, and when you go to the ladies' room on the train you tie the apron around your waist and then you have your brush and comb and hairpins and tooth brush and washrag all where you can lay your fingers on them in a second of time."

"I got my best tortoise-shell hairpin mixed up with another woman's once, and I never recovered it," said Mrs. Morton meditatively.

"It wouldn't have happened if you'd been supplied with a bag like this," said her mother.

"Mademoiselle's silk wrap must be grey to match her other Red Cross equipment," said Mrs. Emerson, "but I don't see why the chintz things shouldn't be as gay as you like."

"Pink roses would be most becoming to her style of beauty," murmured Roger who had come in.

"I don't know but pink roses would be becoming enough for slippers," agreed Ethel Blue so seriously that every one laughed.

"Let's get pink flowered chintz," said Ethel Brown. "You make the soft kind and I'll make the stiff kind and Dorothy'll make the apron and Helen will make the kimono. Who's got any more ideas?"

"I have," contributed Roger. "I'll make a case for her manicure set. I haven't got time this week unfortunately to tool the leather but I'll make a plain one that will be useful if it isn't as pretty as I can do."

"What shape will it be?"

"I got part of my idea from Grandfather Emerson's spectacle case that I was examining the other day. Ethel Blue's case for the soft slippers is going to be something like it."

"Two pieces of leather rounded at the lower corners and stitched together at the sides and with a flap to shut in the contents?" guessed Dorothy.

"Correct. I shall make the case about four inches long when it's closed."

"That means that you'd have one strip four inches long and the other, the one with the flap, six inches long."

"Once more correct, most noble child. It will be a liberal two inches wide, a bit more in this instance because I'm not much of a sewer and I want to be sure that I'm far enough from the edge to make it secure."

"You don't try to turn it inside out, do you?"

"No, ma'am. Not that mite of an object. You fit a tiny pasteboard slide into the case. Cover it with velvet or leather or a scrap of Ethel Blue's chintz—"

"'Rah for cotton," cheered Dorothy.

"—and on one side of this division you slip in the scissors and the file and the tweezers or the orange stick and on the other a little buffer with a strap handle that doesn't take up any room."

"How in the world do you happen to be so up in manicure articles?" queried Helen, amazed at his knowledge.

"Nothing strange about that," returned Roger. "Aunt Louise showed me hers the other day when I was talking to her about making one for just this occasion. Aha!"

"You could make the same sort of case without the pasteboard partition, for a tiny sewing kit," offered Ethel Blue, "and one of the envelope shape will hold soap leaves."

"I'd like to suggest a couple of shirtwaist cases," said Mrs. Smith. "They are made of dotted Swiss muslin that takes up next to no room and washes like a handkerchief. You'd better make Mademoiselle's of colored muslin or of colored batiste for she won't want to be bothered with thinking about laundry any oftener than she has to."

"What shape are the bags?"

Shirtwaist Case Shirtwaist Case

"Find out whether she will take an American suitcase or a bag. In either case measure the size of the bottom. Take a piece of muslin twice the size and lay it flat. Fold over the edges till they meet in the centre. Then stitch the tops across, on the inside, of course, and hem the slit, and turn them right side out and that's all there is to it. They keep waists or neckwear apart from the other clothing in one's bag and fresher for the separation."

"Since I have my hand in with knitting," said Grandmother, "I believe I'll contribute a pair of bed-shoes. They're so simple that any one who can knit a plain strip can do them."

"Let's have the receipt."

"Cast on stitches enough to run the length of the person's foot. Fifty will be plenty for any woman and more than enough for Mademoiselle's tiny foot. It's well to have the shoe large, though. Knit ahead until you have a strip six inches high. Then cast off from one end stitches enough to make four inches and go ahead with the remainder for four inches more."

"That sounds funny to me," observed Ethel Brown. "Not exactly the shape of my dainty pedestal."

"You'll have made a square with a square out of one corner like this piece of paper. Now fold it along the diagonal line from the tip of the small square to the farthest edge of the big square and sew up all the edges except those of the small square. That leaves a hole where you put your foot in. Crochet an edge there to run a ribbon in—and you're done."

"I'm going to run the risk of Mademoiselle's laughing at me and give her a folding umbrella," said Mrs. Morton. "It will fit into her bag and at least she can use it until she goes to the front."

"All this sounds to me like a good outfit for any woman who is going to travel," observed Helen. "I'm almost moved to sail myself!"

CHAPTER VIII

THE RED CROSS NURSE SETS SAIL

THE girls' cheeks were rosy and their hair was tangled by the wind as Helen and the rest of the U. S. C. left the car at West Street and made their way to the French Line Pier. Roger was heading the flock of Mortons, Mrs. Smith was with Dorothy, the Hancocks had come from Glen Point, more for the fun of seeing a sailing than to say "Good-bye" to Mademoiselle, whom they hardly; knew. The Watkinses were accompanied by their elder brother, Edward, a young doctor.

There was a mighty chattering as the party hastened down the pier. A mightier greeted them when they reached the gang plank.

"Every Frenchman left in New York must be here saying 'Good-bye' to somebody!" laughed Tom as his eye fell on the throng pressing on to the boat over a narrow plank across which passengers who had already said their farewells were leaving, and stewards were carrying cabin trunks.

"Only one passerelle for all that!" exclaimed a plump Frenchman whose age might be guessed by the fashion of his moustache and goatee which declared him to be a follower of Napoleon III. He was carrying a bouquet in one hand and kissing the other vehemently to the lady on the deck who was to be made the recipient of the flowers as soon as her admirer could manage to squeeze himself down the over-crowded gang plank.

Taxis driving up behind the U. S. C. young people discharged their occupants upon the agitated scene. All sorts of messages were being sent across to friends on the other side, many of them shouted from pier to deck with a volubility that was startling to inexperienced French students.

It was quite twenty minutes before the Club succeeded in filing Indian fashion across the passerelle. They were met almost at once by Mademoiselle, for she had been watching their experiences from the vessel.

"Before you say 'Good-bye' to me," she said hurriedly, "I want you to go over the ship. I have special permission from the Captain. You must go quickly. There are not many minutes, you were so long in coming on."

She gave them over to the kind offices of a "mousse" or general utility boy, who in turn introduced them to a junior officer who examined their permit as "friends of Mademoiselle Millerand" and then conveyed them to strange corners whose existence they never had guessed.

First they peeked into a cabin which was one of the handsomest on the ship but whose small size brought from Ethel Brown the comment that it was a "stingy" little room. The reading and writing rooms she approved, however, as being cheerful enough to make you forget you were seasick. A lingering odor of the food of yester-year seemed to cling about the saloon and to mingle with a whiff of oil from the engine room that had assailed them just before they entered. People were saying farewells here with extraordinary impetuosity, men embracing each other with a fervor that made the less demonstrative Americans smile. One group was looking over a pile of letters on the table to see if absent friends had sent some message to catch them before they steamed.

Below were other staterooms, rows upon rows of them, and yet others below those. By comparison with the fragrances here that in the saloon seemed a breeze from Araby the Blest.

From above the party had looked down on the engines whose huge steel arms slid almost imperceptibly over each other as if they were slowly, slowly preparing to spring at an unseen foe; as if they knew that great waves would try to still them, the mighty workers of the great ship. A gentle breathing now seemed to stir them, but far, far down below the waterline the stokers were feeding the animal with the fuel that was to give him energy to contend with storms and winds and come out victor. Half naked men, their backs gleaming in the light from the furnaces, threw coal into the yawning mouth. The heat was intense, and the Ethels turned so pale that young Doctor Watkins hurried them into the open air. Helen was not sorry to breathe the coolness of the Hudson again and even the boys drew a long breath of relief, though they did not admit that they had been uncomfortable.

"Mademoiselle Millerand awaits you in the tea room," explained the young officer, and he conducted them to a portion of the deck where passengers could sit in the open, or, on cold or windy days, behind glass and watch the sea and the passengers pacing by.

Mademoiselle greeted them with shining eyes. During their absence there had been some farewells that had been difficult.

"You have seen everything?" she inquired pleasantly. "Then you must have some lemonade with me before you go," and she gave an order that soon brought a trayful of glasses that tinkled cheerfully.

"We are not going to be sentimental," she insisted. "This is just 'Good-bye,' and thank you many times for being so good to me at school, and many, many times more for the bundle that is in my room to surprise me. I shall open it when the Statue of Liberty is out of sight, when I can no more see my adopted land. Then shall I think of all of you and of your Club for Service."

"Where do you expect to be sent, Mademoiselle?" inquired Doctor Watkins as the party walked toward the passerelle over which they must somehow contrive to make their way before they could touch foot upon the pier.

"To Belgium, I think. My brother is a surgeon and I have a distant relative in the ministry—"

"What—the Millerand?"

Mademoiselle smiled and nodded.

"So probably I shall be sent wherever I wish—and my heart goes but to Belgium. It is natural."

"Yes, it is natural. May you have luck," he cried holding out his hand.

"Mademoiselle is going to Belgium," he told the young people who were awaiting their turn at the gang-plank.

They gazed at her with a sort of awe. Tales of war's horrors were common in the ears of all of them, and it was difficult to believe that the slight figure standing there so quietly beside them would see with her own eyes the uptorn fields and downfallen cottages, the dying men and the miserable women and children they had seen only in imagination.

"Oh," gasped Ethel Blue; "oh! Belgium! Oh, Mademoiselle, won't you send us back a Belgian baby? The Club would love to take care of it! Wouldn't we? Wouldn't we?" she cried turning from one to another with glittering eyes.

"We would, Mademoiselle, we would," cried every one of them; and as the big ship was warped out of the pier they waved their handkerchiefs and their hands and cried over and over, "Send us a Belgian baby!"

"Un bébé belge! Ces chers enfants!" ejaculated a motherly Frenchwoman who was weeping near them. "A Belgian baby! These dear children."

And then, to James's horror, she kissed him, first on one cheek and then on the other.

CHAPTER IX

PLANNING THE U. S. C. "SHOW"

IT was becoming more and more evident every day to the president of the United Service Club that it must have more money than was at its disposal at the moment or it would not be able to carry out its plans. Already it owed to Mrs. Morton a sum that Helen knew was larger than her mother could lend them conveniently. All of Grandfather Emerson's donation had gone to provide knitting needles and yarn for the occupants of the Old Ladies' Home, and the Club's decision to lay itself under no financial obligation to people outside of the immediate families of the members had obliged her to refuse a few small gifts that had been offered.

All the members of the Club were working hard to earn money beyond their allowances and every cent was going into the Club's exchequer. Roger was faithful in his attention to the three furnaces he had undertaken to care for, though he was not above a feeling of relief that the weather was continuing so mild that he had not yet had to keep up fires continuously in any of them. James still drove his father, though the doctor threatened him with discharge almost every day because of his habit of cutting corners. The girls were carrying out their plans for money-making, and Della had secured another order for stenciled curtains which Dorothy and Ethel Brown filled.

What with school and working for the orphans and working for the Club treasury these were busy days, and Helen felt that something must be done at once to provide a comparatively large sum so that their indebtedness might be paid off and the pressure upon each one of them would not be so heavy.

Helen and James were going over the Club accounts one Saturday before the regular meeting. A frown showed Helen's anxiety and James's square face looked squarer and more serious than ever as he saw the deficit piled against them.

"It's high time we gave that entertainment we talked about so much when we began this thing," he growled. "People will have forgotten all about it and we'll have to advertise it all over again."

"That'll be easy enough if we make use of some of the small children in some way. All their relatives near and far will know all about it promptly and they'll all come to see how the kiddies perform," said Helen wisely, though her look of perplexity continued.

"Let's bring it up at the meeting right now. I don't believe we can do anything better this afternoon than plan out our show and decide who and what and where."

"'Where' is answered easily enough—the hall of the schoolhouse. 'Who' and 'what' require more thought."

It turned out, however, that every one had been thinking of stunts to do himself or for some one else to do, so that the program did not take as much time as if the subject had not been lying in their minds for several weeks.

"At the beginning," said Ethel Blue, "I think some one ought to get up and tell what the Club is trying to do—all about the war orphans and the Santa Claus Ship."

"Wouldn't Grandfather Emerson be a good one to do that?"

"I don't think we want to have any grown people in our show," was Helen's opinion. "If we bring them in then the outside people will expect more from us because they'll think that we've been helped and it won't be fair to us or to our grown-ups."

"That's so," agreed Tom from the depths of a lifetime of experience of the ways of people in church entertainments. "Let's do every single thing ourselves if we can, and I believe the audience will like it better even if it isn't all as O. K. as it would be if we had a grown-up or two to help pull the oars."

"The first question before us, then, is who will do this explanation act that Ethel Blue suggests?"

There was a dead silence. No one wanted to offer. There seemed no one person on whom the task fell naturally unless—"The Club was Ethel Blue's idea," went on Helen. "Isn't she the right one to explain it?" and "The president of the Club ought to tell about it," said Ethel Blue. Both girls spoke at once.

There was unanimous laughter.

"'Ayther is correct,'" quoted Roger. "I think Helen is the proper victim."

"Yes, indeed," Ethel Blue supported him so earnestly that every one laughed again.

"You see, no one knows about its being Ethel Blue's idea and that would take a lot more explaining or else it would seem that there was no good reason for the president's not acting as showman and introducing her freaks to the audience."

"'Speak for yourself, John!' I'm no freak!" declared James. "I think Helen's the right one to make the introduction, though."

Helen shivered.

"I must say I hate to do it," she said, "but we all agreed when we went into this that we'd do what came up, no matter whether we liked it or not, so here goes Number on the program," and she wrote on her pad, beneath an elaborate

PROGRAM

which she had been drawing and decorating as she talked.

. Explanatory address. Helen Morton.

"Now, then," queried Ethel Brown, "what next?"

"Music, if there's any one to tootle for the ladies," said Roger.

"Dorothy's the singer."

"Oh, I couldn't sing all alone," objected Dorothy shrinkingly. "But Mother said she'd drill a chorus of children and I wouldn't mind doing the solo part with a lot of others on the stage with me."

"How about a chorus in costume?" asked Helen.

"What kind of costume?"

"Oh, I don't know—something historical, perhaps."

"Why not the peasant costumes of the countries in the war?" suggested Ethel Blue. "We're working for the children and we'll have a child or two from each country."

"A sort of illustration of Helen's speech," said Tom.

"They might sing either the national songs of their countries or children's songs," said Dorothy.

"Or both, with you dressed as Columbia and singing the Star Spangled Banner at the end."

"La, la! Fine!" commended Margaret. "Put down Number , Helen, 'Songs by War Orphans.' We can work out the details later, or leave them to Dorothy and her mother."

"I've been thinking that we might as well utilize some of the folk dances that we learned at Chautauqua last summer," said Ethel Brown. "Wouldn't Number be a good spot to put in the Butterfly Dance?"

"That was one of the prettiest dances at the Exhibition," said James. "Let's have it."

"Margaret and I are too tall for it, but you four young ones know it and you can teach four more girls easily enough."

"We'll ask them to-morrow at school," said Dorothy, "and we'll have a rehearsal right off. Mother will play for us and it won't take any time at all."

"The costumes won't take any time, either. Any white dress will do and the wings are made by strips of soft stuff—cheese cloth or something even softer, pale blue and pink and green and yellow. They're fastened at the shoulders and a loop goes over the wrist or the little finger so the arms can keep them waving."

"Do you remember the steps, Dorothy?"

"They're very simple, but almost anything that moves sort of swimmingly will do."

"There's Number , then," decided Dorothy. "Now the boys ought to appear."

"Yes, what have you three been planning to throw us in the shade?" inquired Della.

"I've got a fancy club-swinging act that's rather good," admitted Roger modestly.

"You have?" asked Tom in surprise. "So have I. What's yours?"

"Come over here and I'll tell you," and the two boys retired to a corner where they conferred. It was evident, from their burst of laughter and their exclamations that they highly approved of each other's schemes.

"We've decided that we won't tell you what our act is," they declared when they came back to the broken meeting. "We'll surprise you as well as the rest of the audience."

"Meanies," pronounced Ethel Brown. "Helen, put down 'Number , Club Swinging by Two Geese!'"

"Not geese," corrected Tom, with a glance at Roger, who made a sign of caution.

"What next?" queried the president.

"Let's have some of the small children now. Our honorary member ought to be on the card," said Della.

"Are you sure he wouldn't be afraid?" asked Tom of Dicky's brethren.

"Not Dicky," they shrieked in concert.

"I saw a pretty stunt in town the other evening. It was done by grown people but it would be dear with little kids," urged Della, her round face beaming with the joy of her adaptation of the idea. "It was a new kind of shadow dance."

"Pshaw, that's old," declared Tom with brotherly curtness.

"It wasn't done behind a sheet. That's the old way—"

"A mighty good way, too," supported James stoutly. "I've seen some splendid pantomimes done on a sheet—'Red Riding Hood' and 'Jack the Giant Killer,' and a lot more."

"This is much cunninger," insisted Della. "Instead of a sheet there's a dull, light blue curtain hung across the stage. The light is behind it, but the actors are in front of it."

"Then you don't see their shadows."

"You see themselves in silhouette against the blue. There is a net curtain down between them and the audience and it looks like moonlight with elves and fairies playing in it."

"It would be hard to train Dicky to be a fairy," decided Ethel Blue so gravely that all the others laughed.

"I was thinking that it would be fun to have Dicky and some other children dressed like pussy cats and rabbits and dogs, and playing about as if they were frisking in the moonlight."

"Why not have them do a regular little play like 'Flossy Fisher's Funnies' that have been coming out in the Ladies' Home Journal?" screamed Ethel

Brown, electrified at the growth of the idea. "Take almost any one of them and get the children to play the little story it tells and I don't see why it wouldn't be too cunning for words."

"What kind of stories?" asked James who liked to understand.

"I don't remember any one exactly but they are something like this;—Mr. Dog goes fishing on the bank of the stream. A strip of pasteboard cut at the top into rushes will give the effect of a brook, you know. He pulls up a fish with a jerk that throws it over his head. Pussy Cat is waiting just behind him. She seizes the fish and runs away with it. Mr. Dog runs after her. The cat jumps over a wheelbarrow, but the dog doesn't see it and gets a fall—and so on."

"I can see how it would be funny with little scraps of kids," pronounced Tom. "Who'll train them?"

"I'll do that," offered Ethel Brown. "Dicky's always good with me and if he understands the story he'll really help teach the others."

"Pick out a simple 'Flossy Fisher' or make up an easy story with plenty of action," advised Margaret. "The chief trouble you'll have is to make the children stay apart on the stage. They'll keep bunching up and spoiling the silhouettes if you aren't careful."

"Number . Silhouettes," wrote Helen on her pad. "What's Number ?"

"I don't know whether you'll approve of this," offered Dorothy rather shyly, "but when I was at the Old Ladies' Home the other day I thought they made a real picture knitting away there in the sunshine in their sitting room. Do you think some of them could be induced to come to the schoolhouse and make a tableau?"

"Fine!" commended Helen.

"You could have it a picture of sentiment, such as Dorothy had in mind, I judge," said Tom, "or you could turn it into a comic by having some one sing 'Sister Susie's Sewing Shirts for Soldiers.'"

"What's that?"

"A stay-at-home war song they're singing in England. It's funny because it's so full of S's that it's almost impossible to sing it without a mistake. I think it would be better, though, to have the old ladies just knitting away. After all, it's sympathy with the orphans we want to arouse."

"Couldn't we have a tableau within a tableau—a picture at the back placed with the figures posed behind a net curtain so that they'd be dimmed—a picture of some of the Belgian orphans refugeeing into Holland or something of that sort?"

"If Mademoiselle would only send us right off that Belgian baby that James got kissed for we'd have an actual exhibit," said Roger.

James made a face at the memory of the unexpected caress he had earned unwittingly, but he approved highly of the addition to the picture of the old ladies.

"They're thinking about the orphans as they knit—and there are the orphans," he said, and even his sister Margaret smiled at the approbation with which he looked on a tableau that left nothing to the imagination.

"Number is settled, then. Why can't we have the minuet for Number ?"

"Good. All of us here know it so we shan't need to rehearse much."

"On that small stage four couples will be plenty, I say," offered Roger.

"I think so, too. Eight would make it altogether too crowded," declared Helen. "That means that four of us girls will dance—we can decide which ones later—and you three boys, and we'll only have to train one new boy."

"What's the matter with George Foster? His sister is a dancing teacher and perhaps he knows it already."

"He's the best choice we can make. We want to get this thing done just as fast as we can for several reasons," continued Helen. "In the first place any entertainment goes off more snappily if the fun of doing it isn't all worn off by too many rehearsals."

"Correct," agreed Tom. "Remember that Children's Symphony we exhausted ourselves on for a month last winter, Della?"

Della did and expressed her memories with closed eyes and out-stretched hands.

"If each one of us makes himself and herself responsible for having his own part perfect and the stunts that he's drilling others in as nearly perfect as he can, then I don't see why we need more than ten days for it."

"Especially as we know all the dances now and the Old Ladies' Home tableau won't take much preparation."

"Have we got enough numbers on the program, Helen?"

"I think we ought to end with a long thing of some sort."

"We'll never pull off the show if you try to stick in a play," growled James.

"Not a play, but I was reading Browning's 'Pied Piper of Hamelin' the other day and it can easily be made workable with just a little speaking and some pantomime. Two or three rehearsals ought to do it."

"All right, then. Your sufferings be on your head."

"You'll all back me up, won't you?"

"We'll do whatever you tell us, if that's what you want."

"Read us the whole program, Madam President," begged Dorothy.

"Here you are; I've changed the order a little:

PROGRAM

. Address, Helen Morton.

. Songs by War Orphans, led by Dorothy Smith.

. Butterfly Dance.

. Club Swinging by Roger Morton and Thomas Watkins.

. Knitting for the War Orphans by Ladies from the Old Ladies' Home.

. Silhouettes by Dicky Morton and other Juniors.

. Minuet.

. "The Pied Piper."

"If I do say it as shouldn't, having had a modest part in its construction," remarked Roger complacently, "that's a good program."

"Do you know," added Margaret earnestly, "I think so too."

So, after discussion of details concerning responsibility and rehearsals, and the appointment of a publicity committee consisting of the officers of the Club plus Roger, the meeting adjourned.

CHAPTER X

THE EVENTFUL EVENING

IF the U. S. C.'s had thought themselves busy before they undertook their entertainment they concluded as they rushed from one duty to another in the ten days of preparation for that function that they had not learned the A B C of busy-ness. Mrs. Morton always insisted that, whatever was on foot, school work must not be slighted.

"Your education is your preparation for life," she said. "While you are young you must lay down a good foundation for the later years to build on. You know what happens when a foundation is poor."

They did. A building in Rosemont had fallen into a heap of ruins not long before, to the shame of the contractor who had put in poor work.

So all the school duties were attended to faithfully, and the out-of-door time was not skimped though the out-of-door time was largely devoted to doing errands connected with the "show," and the home lessons were learned as thoroughly as usual. But sewing went by the board for ten days except such sewing as was necessary for the making of costumes.

"Here's a chance for your Club to try out some of Roger's ideas of system," said Grandfather Emerson as he listened to the plans which were always on the lips of the club members whenever he met them.

"I think we're doing it all pretty systematically," Helen defended. "Each one of us is responsible for doing certain things and our work doesn't overlap. When we come together for a general rehearsal I believe we're going to find that all the parts will fit together like a cut-out puzzle."

Costume for Butterfly Dance Costume for Butterfly Dance

Mr. Emerson said that he hoped so in a tone of such doubt that Helen was more than ever determined that all should run smoothly. To that end she made a diplomatic investigation into every number of the program. Every one she found to be going on well. Her own address was already blocked out in her mind. Dorothy had taken bodily a singing class that Mrs. Smith had started at the Rosemont Settlement and, with the knowledge of singing that the children already had, they soon were drilled in their special songs and in the motions that enlivened them. Mrs. Smith and Dorothy were also preparing the costumes and they reported that the mothers of the children were helping, some of them providing actual peasant costumes that had come from the old country.

With four girls who already knew the butterfly dance the drilling of another quartette was swiftly done, and the Ethels were willing to put their flock of butterflies on the stage four days after they had begun to practice. Because every one of them had a white dress their costumes required almost no work beyond the cutting lengthwise of a yard and a quarter of cheesecloth. When they had gathered one end and attached the safety pin which was to fasten it to the shoulder, and gathered the other end and sewed on a loop which was to go over the little finger—all of which took about five minutes—that costume was finished.

About the boys' club swinging Helen could not obtain any information beyond the assurance that all was well. With that she had to content herself.

The old ladies at the Home were delighted to be able to help and also delighted at the excitement of taking part in the entertainment. They voted for the trio who should represent them in the tableaux and generously selected three who were the most handicapped of all of them. One was lame and always sat with her crutch beside her; one was blind, though her fast flying fingers did not betray it; and the third lived in a wheel-chair. They demurred strongly to their companions' choice, but the other old ladies were insistent and the appointees could not resist the fun. Mr. Emerson agreed to provide transportation for them, wheel-chair and all, and Doctor Hancock was to send over a wagonette from Glen Point so that the rest of the inmates of the Home might take advantage of the tickets that some mysterious giver had sent to every one of them. For the inner picture Dicky and two of his kindergarten friends were to be posed, clad in rags.

"It's no trouble to provide Dicky with a ragged suit," said Mrs. Morton. "The difficulty is going to be to make him look serious and poorly fed."

"A little artistic shading under his eyes and on his cheeks will make his plumpness disappear. I'll 'make up' the children," offered Mrs. Emerson.

Most difficult of all were the silhouettes. This was because the children who were to take part were so tiny that they could not quite remember the sequence of the story they were to act out. There were moments when the Ethels were almost disposed to give up the youngsters and try the shadows with larger children.

"The little ones make so much cunninger cats and dogs than the bigger children I don't want to do it unless we have to," said Ethel Brown, and they found at last that perseverance won the day. Here, too, the children's mothers helped with the costumes, and turned out a creditable collection of animal coverings, not one of them with a bit of fur.

"They're another help to your cotton crusade," Ethel Blue told Dorothy.

Grey flannelette made a soft maltese pussy; the same material in brown covered a dog; a white coat splashed with brown spots out of the family coffee pot was the covering of another Fido, while another white garment stained with black and yellow ornamented a tortoise-shell cat. The rabbits all wore white.

As with the butterfly dance so many of the performers knew the minuet that it needed only two rehearsals. The new boy worked in without any trouble and was so graceful and dignified that the U. S. C. boys found themselves emulating his excellent manner.

Helen herself took charge of "The Pied Piper" and so few were the speaking parts and so short and so natural the pantomime that she drilled her company in three rehearsals, though she herself worked longer in private over the manipulation of certain stage "properties," and had one or two special sessions with Dr. Edward Watkins who was to take the principal part.

Friday evening was chosen for the performance. The Rosemont young people usually had their evening festivities on Fridays because they could sit up later than usual without being disturbed about school work the next morning. The special Friday proved to be clear with a brilliant moon and the old ladies driving over from the Home felt themselves to be out on a grand lark. Evidently the boys had done their publicity work thoroughly, for not only did they see a goodly number of Rosemont people approaching the schoolhouse, but, just as they drove up to the door, a special car from Glen Point stopped to let off a crowd of friends of the Hancocks who had come over to see "what the children were doing for the war orphans."

The school hall held people and no seats were reserved except those for the old ladies. They found themselves in front where they could see well and where they were near enough to appreciate the care with which the edge of the platform was decorated. That had been Margaret Hancock's work and she had remembered the success of the Service Club in preparing the platform for the Old First Night exercises at Chautauqua.

Tom had insisted that the Club should go to the extra expense of having tickets printed. James had objected.

"This old treasury of ours is almost an empty box," he growled. "We can't afford to spend cold cash on printing."

"It will pay in the end, believe me," insisted Tom slangily. "You know there are always a lot of people who think they'll go to a show and then at the last minute think they won't if something more amusing turns up. If you sell tickets beforehand you've got their contribution to the cause even if they don't appear themselves."

"Tom's right," agreed Margaret. "They won't mind losing so small a sum as a quarter if they don't go."

"And they'd think it was too small an amount to bother themselves about by hunting up the treasurer and paying it in if they didn't have a ticket," said Roger.

"And there are some people who'd be sure to come and swell the audience just because they had spent a quarter on a ticket," said Ethel Brown.

"What does the president think?" asked Ethel Blue.

Helen agreed with Tom and the tickets were printed. After all they came to only a small sum and Roger, peeking through a hole in the curtain, saw with satisfaction that if there were going to be any vacant seats at all they would not be many. When one of the old ladies turned about just before the curtain went up she saw a solid room behind her and people standing against the wall.

There was music before the curtain rose. This enrichment of the program was a surprise to the performers themselves. Young Doctor Edward Watkins had become so interested in the United Service Club when he met them at the French Line Pier that he had insisted on helping with their work for the orphans.

"If Mademoiselle really sends you that Belgian baby you may need a special physician for it," he said. "So you'd better stand in with one whose practice isn't big enough yet to take all his time."

He said this to Helen when he appeared with Tom and Della on the evening of the performance and announced that not only did he know his part in the "Piper" but he had brought his violin and would be glad to be a part of the orchestra.

"But we haven't an orchestra," objected Helen. "I wish we had."

"Who's going to play for the dances?"

"Aunt Louise."

"Why can't she and I do something at the beginning? It will seem a little less cold than just having the curtain go up without any preliminaries."

Mrs. Smith proved to be delighted to go over with Doctor Watkins the music he had brought and they selected one or two lively bits that would set the mood of the audience for the evening. So Mrs. Morton and the Emersons and the younger members of the cast were greatly surprised to hear an overture from a well-played violin accompanied by the piano. While the applause was dying away the curtain rose on Helen seated at a desk reading from a blank exercise book filled with Ethel Blue's neat writing.

"This is the report of the Secretary of the United Service Club," began Helen when the applause that greeted her appearance had subsided. She was looking very pretty, wearing a straight, plain pink frock and having her hair bound with a narrow pink fillet.

"Perhaps you don't know what the United Service Club is," she went on, and then she told in the simplest manner of the beginning of the Club at Chautauqua the summer before.

"What we're trying to do is to help other people whether we want to or not," she declared earnestly.

A soft laugh went over the audience at this contradictory statement.

"I mean," continued Helen, somewhat confused, "that we mean to do things that will help people even if we don't get any fun out of it ourselves. We want to improve our characters, you see," she added artlessly. "So far we haven't had much chance to improve our characters because all the things that have come our way to do have been things that were great fun—like to-night.

"To-night," she went on earnestly, "you have come here to see a little entertainment that we've gotten up to make some money so that we could send a bigger bundle to the Christmas Ship that is going to sail for Europe early in November. We thought we could make a good many presents for the war orphans but we found that our allowances didn't go as far as we thought they would, although we have a very careful treasurer," she added with a smiling glance at the wings of the stage where James greeted her compliment with a wry face.

"We made a rule that we would make all the money we needed and not accept presents, so this show is the result, and we hope you'll like it. Anyway, we've had lots of fun getting it up."

She bowed her thanks to the applause that greeted her girlish explanation and stepped behind the scenes.

Immediately a gay march sounded from the piano. It was a medley of well-known national songs and in time with its notes a group of children led by Dorothy ran upon the stage. Dorothy stepped to the front and sang a few lines of introduction to the tune of "Yankee Doodle."

"Here we are from Fatherland,

From Russia and from France,

From Japan and from Ireland

We all together dance.

"At home they are not dancing now;

There's war and awful slaughter;

We here in Rosemont make our bow,

Each one Columbia's daughter."

Then a flaxen-haired little girl stepped forward and sang a German folk song and after it she and two other children dressed in German peasant costume danced a merry folk dance. Representatives of the other countries which Dorothy's verses had named sang in turn. Then each group sang its national song, at the end uniting in "The Star Spangled Banner," in which the standing audience joined.

There was a great clapping when the curtain fell, but the managers had decided that there should be no encores, so the curtain merely rose once upon a bowing, smiling group and then fell with a decision that was understood to be final.

"Whatever we do wrong, the thing we must do right," Helen had insisted when she was drilling her performers, "is to have promptness in putting on our 'acts.'"

"That's so," agreed Tom, "there's nothing an audience hates more than to wait everlastingly between 'turns' while whispering and giggling goes on behind the scenes."

As a result of Helen's sternness the butterflies were waiting when the little internationals went off, and, as those of the children who were not to appear again filed quietly down into the audience where they could see the remainder of the performance, waving wings of soft pink and blue and green and yellow fluttered in from the sides. There was nothing intricate about the steps of this pretty dance. There were movements forward and back and to one side and another, with an occasional turn, but the slowly waving hands with their delicate burden of color made the whole effect entirely charming.

When Tom and Roger, jersey clad, stepped on to the stage for the club-swinging act all the other performers were clustered in the wings, for it had roused their curiosity. Evidently Roger was to swing first for he stepped to the front while Tom beckoned to the janitor of the hall who came forward and attached electric light wires to a plug in the edge of the platform. Tom made a connection with wires that ran up under the back of Roger's jersey and down his sleeves and through holes bored into his clubs, and then he stepped forward to the front.

"While Roger Morton is swinging his clubs the lights of the hall will be turned off," he explained. "I mention it so that no one will be startled when they go out."

Out they went, and in a flash Roger's clubs, made of red and white striped cotton stretched over wire frames which covered electric light bulbs screwed to a sawed-off pair of clubs, were illuminated from within. The beauty of the movements as the clubs flashed here and there in simple or elaborate curves and whirls drew exclamations of enjoyment from the audience.

"That's one of the prettiest stunts I ever saw," exclaimed Doctor Hancock, and Doctor Watkins led the vigorous applause that begged Roger to go on. True to his agreement with Helen, however, Roger stepped aside as soon as he was freed from his apparatus and the lights were turned on once more in the hall, and prepared to help Tom.

It was clear that Tom, too, was not going to do ordinary club-swinging. He took up his position in the centre of the stage and Roger brought forward a box which he deposited beside him. The actors behind the scenes craned their heads forward until they were visible to the audience, so eager were they to see what the box contained.

"My friend, Tom Watkins," said Roger gravely, "is something of a naturalist. In the course of his travels and studies he has come across a curious animal whose chief characteristic is what I may be permitted to call its adhesive power. So closely does it cling to anything to which it attaches itself that it can be detached only with great difficulty. So marked is this peculiarity of the Canis Taurus—"

A peculiar grunt of amusement from certain high school members of the audience interrupted Roger's oration. "Canis, dog; taurus, bull," they whispered.

"—of the Canis Taurus," he went on, "that Watkins has been able to train two of his specimens to do the very remarkable act that you are about to see."

As he ended he threw back the top of the box and there popped up over the edge the infinitely ugly heads of Cupid's two pup's, Amor and Amorette. A howl of laughter greeted their silly, solemn countenances. Tom whistled sharply and they sprang from their narrow quarters and ran to him. He stroked them, and faced them toward the footlights so that their eyes should not be dazzled by seeing them suddenly. Then he began to play with them, pushing them about and shoving them gently with the ravelled ends of two short pieces of knotted rope. When he had teased them for a minute he stood upright and Amor and Amorette were hanging each from a rope! It was a trick he had taught them as soon as their teeth were strong enough.

Slowly he swung them back and forth, and then in semi-circles constantly increasing in sweep, until in a flash they rose over his head and described regular simple Indian club evolutions. Every move was slow and steady with no jerks that would break the dogs' hold and Amor and Amorette held on with a firmness that did credit to their inheritance of jaw muscle and determination.

"Good for the Canis Taurus," laughed Mr. Wheeler, the high school teacher, from the back of the hall as the swinging died rhythmically away.

"Speak to the ladies and gentlemen," commanded Tom as he dropped the ropes and their attachments to the floor. Each dog was still holding firmly to his bit of rope and manifested no desire to part from it. At their master's order, however, they let go of their handles and uttered two sharp barks. Then they picked them up again and trotted off the stage.

All this was so unusual that it aroused the most fervent enthusiasm that had yet been shown. Feet stamped and canes rapped but Tom would do no more than walk on with a dog on each side of him and bow as they barked.

With the announcement of the knitting tableau there was a flutter among the old ladies from the Home. Here was an act in which they felt a personal interest. It was almost embarrassing to be so nearly related to a number on the program!

The curtain rose very slowly to soft music thrilling through the hall. It was a homely scene—just such a room as any one of the old ladies may have had when she still had a home of her own. There was a table with a lamp upon it and around the table were the three old ladies, one with her crutch and one in her wheel chair, and one sitting in the darkness that was daylight to her—the shining of a contented heart. All of them were knitting.

Slowly there grew into view behind them on the wall the picture of the thoughts that were in their minds—the picture of three children, pale, thin, tear-stained, trudging along a weary road. Each one carried a bundle far too heavy for him and each looked unsmilingly out of the frame, though Mrs. Morton breathed a sigh of relief when the touching scene faded and she knew that there was no longer any danger of Dicky's spoiling the effect by a burst of laughter or a genial call to some acquaintance in the audience.

Slowly the curtain fell and the old ladies were lost to view. Then the old ladies in front breathed a sigh of satisfaction. It had been simply perfect!

CHAPTER XI

"SISTER SUSIE'S SEWING SHIRTS FOR SOLDIERS"

WITH the evening well under way Helen was beginning to be relieved of the worry that she had not been able to control, but as the time for the silhouette approached the Ethels became distinctly disturbed. Dicky always was an uncertain element. Because he had behaved like an angel child in the tableau with the old ladies was no assurance that as a pussy cat in the silhouettes he would not raise an uproar which would put to shame any backyard feline of their acquaintance.

Dicky's companions in the animal play were ready behind the scenes and their funny costumes were causing bursts of suppressed mirth as they danced about excitedly. When Dicky finished his tableau he was hurried into his maltese coat and by the time that his Aunt Louise had played the "Owl and the Pussy Cat" and Dorothy had sung it, the blue curtain had been lowered, the light behind it turned on, and between it and the net curtain in front the dogs and the cats and the rabbits frisked happily. In fact the raising of the outside curtain caught them tagging each other about the stage in a manner that was vastly amusing but had nothing to do with the play.

For there was a little play. The Ethels had made it up themselves and it had to do not only with a fisher dog who lost his catch to a robber cat but with a clever rabbit who was chased by both dogs and cats and who took refuge in the rushes on the bank of the stream and was passed by because his pursuers mistook the tips of his ears for rushes. Then they made signs that, wherever he was, if he would come out and join them they should all be friends. He came out and they took paws and danced about in a circle. Against the dull blue background it looked as if the animals were playing in the moonlight, jumping and walking on their hindlegs like the creatures in the fairy books. The small children in the audience were especially pleased with this number and when at the end a boy appeared carrying his schoolbooks and all the animals fell into line behind him and walked off demurely to school it was so like what happens at the end of the holidays that they burst into renewed clapping.

The minuet went with the utmost smoothness. Doctor Watkins added his violin to the piano's playing of the Mozart music from "Don Giovanni" and the picturesquely dressed figures stepped and bowed and courtesied with grace and precision. Helen danced with Tom, Margaret with Roger, Ethel Brown with James, and Ethel Blue with the new boy, George Foster. The girls all wore ruffled skirts with paniers elaborately bunched over them, and they had their hair powdered. The boys wore knee breeches, long-tailed coats, and white wigs. On the wall hung an old portrait of a Morton ancestor. A spinet stood at one side of the room which the stage represented. The whole atmosphere was that of a day long gone by.

After this number was done Doctor Watkins appeared before the curtain.

"I am asked by the president of the United Service Club," he said, "to tell you that there will be an interval of ten minutes between the minuet and the next offering of the program. During that time I am going to sing you a song that the English soldiers are singing. It isn't a serious song, for the soldiers are hearing enough sad sounds without adding to them. I may make some mistakes in singing it—you'll understand why in a moment."

At a nod from him, Mrs. Smith broke into the opening notes of "Sister Susie's Sewing Shirts for Soldiers," and by the time the doctor had finished the second stanza the audience was humming the chorus. "Come on," he cried. "I did make some mistakes. See if you can do better," and he led the tune for the four lines that announced,—

"Sister Susie's sewing shirts for soldiers.

Such skill at sewing shirts our shy young sister Susie shows,

Some soldiers send epistles, say they'd sooner sleep in thistles

Than the saucy, soft, short shirts for soldiers Sister Susie sews."

Everybody laughed and laughed and tried to sing and laughed again.

When the chorus was over, Doctor Watkins dashed into the Allies' song, "Tipperary," and followed it by "Deutschland ueber Alles." Then he taught the audience the words of "The Christmas Ship" and they quickly caught the air and soon were singing,—

"Hurrah, hurrah for the Christmas Ship

As it starts across the sea

With its load of gifts and its greater load

Of loving sympathy.

Let's wave our hats and clap our hands

As we send it on its trip;

May many a heart and home be cheered

By the gifts in the Christmas Ship."

Edward had a good voice and he sang with so much spirit that every one enjoyed his unexpected addition to the evening's pleasure.

A bell behind the scenes announced that "The Pied Piper of Hamelin" was ready and the curtain rose on the room in the Town Hall of Hamelin in which the Corporation held its meetings. Dorothy, whose voice was clear and far-reaching, stood just below the stage at one side and read the explanation of what had been happening in the city.

Hamelin Town's in Brunswick,

By famous Hanover city;

The river Weser, deep and wide,

Washes its wall on the southern side;

A pleasanter spot you never spied;

But, when begins my ditty,

Almost five hundred years ago,

To see the townsfolk suffer so

From vermin, was a pity,

Rats!

They fought the dogs and killed the cats,

And bit the babies in the cradles,

And ate the cheeses out of the vats,

And licked the soup from the cooks' own ladles,

Split open the kegs of salted sprats

Made nests inside men's Sunday hats,

And even spoiled the women's chats

By drowning their speaking

With shrieking and squeaking

In fifty different sharps and flats.

At last the people in a body

To the Town Hall came flocking.

At this point the reading stopped and the action began. Roger, dressed as the Mayor in his mother's red flannel kimono banded with white stripes to which he had attached tiny black tails to give the effect of ermine, stalked in first. He wore a look of deep anxiety. Behind him came James and two of Roger's high school friends who represented members of the Corporation. They also were dressed in red robes but they did not attempt to equal the ermine elegance of the Mayor.

After the Mayor and Corporation came a body of the townspeople. They all appeared thoroughly enraged and as the city fathers took their seats at the council table in the centre of the room they railed at them.

First Citizen. Tom, in rough brown jacket and baggy knee breeches, with long brown stockings and low shoes. He frowned savagely and growled in disgust. "'Tis clear our Mayor's a noddy!"

Second Citizen. George Foster, dressed like Tom.

"And as for our Corporation—shocking,

To think we buy gowns lined with ermine

For dolts that can't or won't determine

What's best to rid us of our vermin!"

Third Citizen. Another high school boy. He was bent like a withered old man and spoke in a squeaky voice.

"You hope because you're old and obese,

To find in the furry civic robe ease?"

First Citizen.

"Rouse up, sirs! Give your brains a racking

To find the remedy we're lacking,

Or, sure as fate, we'll send you packing."

The Mayor.

"For a guilder I'd my ermine gown sell,

I wish I were a mile hence."

First Member of the Corporation. James.

"It's easy to bid one rack one's brain—

I'm sure my poor head aches again,

I've scratched it so and all in vain."

Second Member of the Corporation.

"Oh, for a trap, a trap, a trap."

At this instant came a rap on the door. Helen did it, and a cry came from The Mayor.

"Bless us, what's that?"

First Member.

"Only a scraping of shoes on the mat?

Anything like the sound of a rat

Makes my heart go pit-a-pat!"

The Mayor.

"Come in!"

In answer to this permission there entered Edward Watkins as the Pied Piper. He had dashed around to the back and slipped into his coat and Mrs. Emerson had painted his face while the first words of the poem were being read. He was tall and thin with light hair, yet a swarthy complexion. He wore a queer long coat, half yellow and half red and around his neck a scarf of red and yellow in stripes to which was attached a tiny flute with which his fingers played as if he were eager to pipe upon it. He smiled winningly and the people crowded in the council chamber whispered, wondering who he was and why his attire was so curious.

First Citizen.

"It's as my great-grandsire

Starting up at the Trump of Doom's tone,

Had walked this way from his painted tombstone."

The Pied Piper Edward Watkins advanced to the council table.

"Please your honors, I'm able

By means of a secret charm to draw

All creatures living beneath the sun,

That creep or swim or fly or run,

After me so as you never saw!

And I chiefly use my charm

On creatures that do people harm,

The mole and toad and newt and viper;

And people call me the Pied Piper.

Yet, poor piper as I am,

In Tartary I freed the Cham,

Last June from his huge swarms of gnats;

I eased in Asia the Nizam

Of a monstrous brood of vampire bats:

And as for what your brain bewilders

If I can rid your town of rats

Will you give me a thousand guilders?"

The Mayor and Corporation Together.

"One? Fifty thousand!"

Then The Piper walked slowly across the stage, erect and smiling, and he piped a strange, simple tune on his flute. As he disappeared at one side the stage was darkened and at the back appeared a picture such as had been used in the tableau of the old ladies knitting. The Mayor and the Corporation and the townsfolk turned their back to the audience and gazed out through this window. Across it passed first The Piper still piping, and after him a horde of rats. They were pasteboard rats and Helen was drawing them across the scene with strings, but they made a very good illusion of the dancing rats that the poet described;

Great rats, small rats, lean rats, brawny rats;

Brown rats, black rats, gray rats, tawny rats.

As the crowd in the room watched they uttered exclamations—"See!" "Look at that one!" "How they follow him!" "He's leading them to the river!" "In they go!" "They're drowning!" "Every one of them!" "Let's ring the bells!"

With faces of delight the townsfolk left the council chamber and from a distance came the muffled ringing of bells of joy.

The Mayor addressed them as they passed out;

"Go and get long poles,

Poke out the nests and block up the holes!

Consult with carpenters and builders,

And leave in our town not even a trace

Of the rats."

The Piper entered suddenly. "First, if you please, my thousand guilders!"

First Member of the Corporation. "A thousand guilders!"

The other members of the Corporation shook their heads in solemn refusal.

The Mayor.

"Our business was done at the river's brink;

We saw with our eyes the vermin sink,

And what's dead can't come to life, I think."

Second Member of the Corporation.

"So, friend, we're not the folks to shrink

From the duty of giving you something for drink,

And a matter of money to put in your poke—"

The Mayor.

"But as for the guilders, what we spoke

Of them, as you very well know, was in joke."

First Member.

"Besides, our losses have made us thrifty.

A thousand guilders! Come, take fifty!"

The Piper looking serious, cried;

"No trifling! I can't wait, beside!

I've promised to visit by dinner time

Bagdat, and accept the prime

Of the Head-Cook's pottage, all he's rich in,

For having left in the Caliph's kitchen,

Of a nest of scorpions no survivor;

With him I proved no bargain-driver,

With you, don't think I'll bate a stiver!

And folks who put me in a passion

May find me pipe after another fashion."

The Mayor.

"How? D'ye think I brook

Being worse treated than a Cook?

Insulted by a lazy ribald

With idle pipe and vesture piebald?

You threaten us, fellow? Do your worst,

Blow your pipe there till you burst!"

Once more the Piper laid the pipe against his lips and blew the strange, simple tune, and from both sides of the stage there came rushing in children of all sizes, boys and girls, flaxen-haired and dark-haired, blue-eyed and brown-eyed. They crowded around him and as he slowly passed off the stage they followed him, dancing and waving their hands and with never a look behind them.

Once more the window at the back opened and across it went the Piper, still fluting, though now he could not be heard by the audience; and behind him still danced the children, blind to the gestures of the Mayor and Corporation who stretched out their arms, beseeching them to return. Terrified, the city fathers made known by gestures of despair that they feared the Piper was leading the children to the river where they would meet the fate of the rats.

Of a sudden they seemed relieved and the picture showed the throng passing out of sight into a cavern on the mountain. Then limped upon the stage a lame boy who had not been able to dance all the way with the children and so was shut out when the mountain opened and swallowed them up. The Corporation crowded around him and heard him say:

Lame Boy.

"It's dull in our town since my playmates left!

I can't forget that I'm bereft

Of all the pleasant sights they see,

Which the Piper also promised me.

For he led us, he said, to a joyous land,

Joining the town and just at hand,

Where waters gushed and fruit trees grew

And flowers put forth a fairer hue,

And everything was strange and new;

The sparrows were brighter than peacocks here,

And their dogs outran our fallow deer,

And honey bees had lost their stings,

And horses were born with eagles' wings;

And just as I became assured

My lame foot would be speedily cured,

The music stopped and I stood still,

And found myself outside the hill,

Left alone against my will,

To go now limping as before,

And never hear of that country more!"

The Mayor and Corporation were grouped around the Lame Boy listening and the citizens at the back leaned forward so as to hear every word. Almost in tears the boy limped from the stage followed slowly by Mayor and Corporation and citizens while Dorothy's clear voice took up the tale.

"Alas, alas for Hamelin!

There came into many a burgher's pate

A text which says that heaven's gate

Opes to the rich at as easy rate

As the needle's eye takes a camel in!

The Mayor sent East, West, North, and South,

To offer the Piper by word or mouth

Wherever it was men's lot to find him,

Silver and gold to his heart's content,

If he'd only return the way he went,

And bring the children behind him.

But when they saw 'twas a lost endeavor,

And Piper and dancers were gone forever,

They made a decree that lawyers never

Should think their records dated duly

If, after the day of the month and year,

These words did not as well appear,

'And so long after what happened here

On the Twenty-second of July,

Thirteen hundred and seventy-six:'

And the better in memory to fix

The place of the children's last retreat,

They called it the Pied Piper's Street—

Where any one playing on pipe or tabor

Was sure for the future to lose his labor.

Nor suffered they hostelry or tavern

To shock with mirth a street so solemn:

But opposite the place of the cavern

They wrote the story on a column,

And on the great church window painted

The same, to make the world acquainted

How their children were stolen away,

And there it stands to this very day.

And I must not omit to say

That in Transylvania there's a tribe

Of alien people who ascribe

The outlandish ways and dress

On which their neighbors lay such stress,

To their fathers and mothers having risen

Out of some subterraneous prison

Into which they were trepanned

Long time ago in a mighty band

Out of Hamelin town in Brunswick land.

But how or why, they don't understand."

At the conclusion of the play, after hearty applause, the audience broke again into the song of the Christmas Ship:

Hurrah, hurrah for the Christmas Ship

As it starts across the sea

With its load of gifts and its greater load

Of loving sympathy.

Let's wave our hats and clap our hands

As we send it on its trip;

May many a heart and home be cheered

By the gifts in the Christmas Ship.

"That's as good a show as if it had been put on by grown-ups," declared a New Yorker who had come out with Doctor Watkins. "It's hard to believe that those kids have done it all themselves."

He spoke to a stranger beside him as they filed out to the music of a merry march played by Mrs. Smith.

"My boy was among them," replied the Rosemont man proudly, "but I don't mind saying I think they're winners!"

That seemed to be every one's opinion. As for the old ladies—the evening was such an event to them that they felt just a trifle uncertain that they had not been transported by some magic means to far away Hamelin town.

"I don't believe I missed a word," said the blind old lady as the horses toiled slowly up the hill to the Home.

"We'll tell you every scene so you'll know how the words fit in," promised the old lady in the wheel chair.

"It will be something to talk about when we're knitting," chuckled the lame old lady brightly, and they all hummed gently,

"Hurrah, hurrah for the Christmas Ship

As it starts across the sea."

CHAPTER XII

JAMES CUTS CORNERS

"VERY creditable, very creditable indeed," repeated Doctor Hancock as he and James stepped into their car to return to Glen Point after packing the old ladies into the wagonette.

Mrs. Hancock and Margaret had gone home by trolley because the doctor had to make a professional call on the way. The moon lighted the road brilliantly and the machine flew along smoothly over the even surface.

"This is about as near flying as a fellow can get and still be only two feet from the earth," said James.

James was quiet and almost too serious for a boy of his age but he had one passion that sometimes got the better of the prudence which he inherited from the Scottish ancestor about whom Roger was always joking him.

That passion was for speed. When he was a very small child he had made it his habit to descend the stairs by way of the rail at the infinite risk of his neck. Once he had run his head through the slats of a chicken coop into which an over-swift hopmobile had thrown him. On roller skates his accidents had been beyond counting because his calculations of distance often seemed not to work out harmoniously with his velocity. It was because Doctor Hancock thought that if the boy had the responsibility for his father's machine and for other people's bones he would learn to exercise proper care, that he had consented to let him become his chauffeur. The plan had seemed to work well, but once in a while the desire to fly got the better of James's discretion.

"Here's where the car gets ahead of the aeroplane," said the doctor. "An aviator would find it dangerous work to skim along only two feet above ground."

"I did want to go up with that airman at Chautauqua last summer!" cried James.

"Why didn't you?"

"Cost too much. Twenty-five plunks."

The doctor whistled.

"Flying high always costs," he said meditatively.

"The Ethels went up. They haven't done talking about it yet. They named the man's machine, so he gave them a ride."

"Good work! Look out for these corners, now. When you've studied physics a bit longer you'll learn why it is that a speeding body can't change its direction at an angle of ninety degrees and maintain its equilibrium unless it decreases its speed."

James thought this over for a while.

"In other words, slow up going round corners," he translated, "and later I'll learn why."

"Words to that effect," replied the doctor mildly.

"Here's a good straight bit," exclaimed James. "You don't care if I let her out, do you? There's nothing in sight."

"Watch that cross road."

"Yes, sir. Isn't this moon great!" murmured James under his breath, excited by the brilliant light and the cool air and the swift motion.

"Always keep your eyes open for these heavy shadows that the moon casts," directed Doctor Hancock. "Sometimes they're deceptive."

"I'll keep in the middle of the road and then the bugaboo in the shadow can see us even if I can't see him," laughed James, the moonlight in his eyes and the rush of wind in his ears.

"There's something moving there! LOOK OUT!" shouted the doctor as a cow strolled slowly out from behind a tree and chewed a meditative cud right across their path. James made a swift, abrupt curve, and did not touch her.

"That was a close one," he whispered, his hands shaking on the wheel.

"It hasn't worried her any," reported his father, looking back. "She hasn't budged and she's still chewing. You did that very well, son. It was a difficult situation."

James flushed warmly. His father was not a man to give praise often so that every word of commendation from him was doubly valued by his children.

"Thank you. I shouldn't like to have it happen every day," James confessed.

They sped on in silence after the cow episode, the boy glad of the chance to steady his nerves in the quiet, the doctor thinking of the case he was to visit in a few minutes.

The patient's house stood on the edge of Glen Point, and James sat in the car resting and watching the machines of the townspeople passing by with gay parties out to enjoy the moonlight. Some, like themselves, had been to Rosemont, and some of his schoolmates waved to him as they passed.

"It was a great show, old man," more than one boy shouted to him.

It had been a good show. He knew it and he was glad that he belonged to a club that really amounted to something. They did things well and they didn't do them well just to show off or to get praise—they had a good purpose behind. He was still thinking about it when his father came out. Doctor Hancock did not talk about his cases, but James had learned that silence meant that there was need for serious thought and that the doctor was in no mood to enter into conversation. When he came out laughing, however, and jumped into the car with a care-free jest, as happened now, James knew that all was going well.

"Now, home, boy," he directed. "Stop at the drug store an instant."

He gave some directions to a clerk who hurried out to them and then they drove on. The moonlight sifted through the trees and flickered on the road. A cool breeze stimulated James's skin to a shiver. On they went, faster and faster. He'd had a mighty good time all the evening, James thought, and Father was a crackerjack.

"LOOK OUT, boy," his father's voice rang through his thoughts. The car struck the curb with a shock that loosened his grasp on the wheel and tossed him into the air. As he flew up he tried to say, "I cut the corner too close that time," but he never knew whether he said it or not, for his voice seemed to fail him and his father could not recall hearing such a remark.

It was quite an hour later when he came to himself. To his amazement he found himself in his own room. The light was shaded, his mother with tears still filling her eyes was beside him, and his father and a young man whom he recognized as the new doctor who had just come to Glen Point, were putting away instruments. He tried to move in the bed and found that his leg was extraordinarily heavy.

"Did I bust my leg?" he inquired briefly.

"You did," returned his father with equal brevity.

"Weren't you hurt?"

"A scratch on the forehead, that's all. Doctor Hanson is going to patch me up now."

The two physicians left the room and James did not know until long after that the scratch required several stitches to mend.

His illness was a severe trial to James. His Scottish blood taught him that his punishment fitted his crime—that he was hurt as a direct result of doing what he knew was likely to bring that result. He said to himself that he was going to take his punishment like a man. But oh, the days were long! The Glen Point boys came in when they thought of it—there was some one almost every day—but the Indian Summer was unusually prolonged and wonderfully beautiful this year, and it was more than any one could ask in reason that the boys should give up outdoors to stay with him. Roger and Helen and the Ethels and Dorothy came over from Rosemont when they could, but their daily work had to be done and they had only a few minutes to stay after the long trolley trip.

"We must think up something for James to do," Mrs. Hancock told Margaret. "He's tired of reading. He can use his hands. Hasn't your Service Club something that he can work on here?" Margaret thought it had, and the result of the conversation was that Mrs. Hancock went to Rosemont on an afternoon car. The Ethels took her to Mrs. Smith's and Dorothy showed her the accumulation for the Christmas Ship that already was making a good showing in the attic devoted to the work.

"These bundles in the packing cases are all finished and ready for their final wrappings," Dorothy explained. "There are dresses and wrappers and sacques and sweaters and all sorts of warm clothing like that."

"And you girls did almost all of it!" exclaimed Mrs. Hancock.

"Helen and Margaret made most of those," said Ethel Brown. "In this box are the knitted articles that are coming in every day now. Most of them are from the Old Ladies' Home so far, but every once in a while somebody else stops and leaves something. We girls don't knit much; it seems to go so slowly."

"I brought one pair of wristers with me and I have another pair almost done," said Mrs. Hancock. "What are these?"

"Those are the boxes the boys have been pasting," said Ethel Blue, picking up one of them. "They began with the large plain ones first—the real packing boxes."

"Here are some that are large enough for a dress."

"We've gathered all the old boxes we could find in our house or in our friends' houses—Margaret must have hunted in your attic for she brought over some a fortnight ago. None of the things we are making will require a box as large as the tailors send out, so we took those boxes and the broken ones that we found and made them over."

"That must have taken a great deal of time."

"The boys paste pretty fast now. Some of them they made to lock together. They didn't need anything but cutting. They got that idea from a tailor's box that Roger found."

Mrs. Hancock examined the flat pasteboard cut so that the corners would interlock.

"The old boxes they cut down. That saves buying new pasteboard. And they've covered some of the battered looking old ones with fresh paper so they look as good as new—"

"And a great deal prettier," said Dorothy.

"We get wall paper at ten cents a roll for the covering," said Ethel Blue. "They have an old-fashioned air that's attractive, Aunt Marion says," and she held up a box covered with wild roses.

"They're lovely! And they must have cost you almost nothing."

"We did these when our treasury was very low. Now we've got almost fifty dollars that we cleared from our entertainment after we paid all our bills and repaid Mother what we owed her," explained Ethel Brown, "so now the boys can get some fresh cardboard and some chintz and cretonne and make some real beauties."

"Is this what James has been doing on Saturdays?"

"James is the best paster of all, he's so careful. He always makes his corners as neat as pins. Sometimes the other boys are careless."

"Then I don't see why James couldn't do some of this at home now. He has altogether too much time on his hands."

"Can't he study yet?"

"He learns his lessons but his father doesn't want him to go to school for at least a fortnight and perhaps not then, so he has long hours with nothing to do except read and it isn't good for him to do that all the time."

"We've got a lot of ideas for pasting that we've been waiting for time and cash to put into operation," said Helen who had come in in time to hear Mrs. Hancock's complaint. "If James could have an old table that you didn't mind his getting sticky, next to his wheel chair he could do a quantity of things that we want very much, and it would help, oh, tremendously."

"Tell me about them," and Mrs. Hancock sat down at once to receive her instructions. Helen brought a sheet of paper and made a list of materials to be bought and drew some of the articles over which she thought that James might be puzzled.

"Some of these ideas we got from magazines," she said, "and some people told us and some we invented ourselves. They aren't any of them very large."

"James will like that. It is more fun to turn off a number of articles. When he has an array standing on his table you must all go over to Glen Point and see them."

"We thought that perhaps you'd let us have a meeting of the U. S. C. at your house one Saturday afternoon, and we could take over some of our work to show James and we could see his, and we could work while we were there," suggested Helen diffidently.

"You're as good as gold to think of it! It will be the greatest pleasure to James. Shall we say this next Saturday?"

The girls agreed that that would be a good time, and Mrs. Hancock went home laden with materials for James's pasting operations and bearing the pleasant news of the coming of the Club to meet with him.

Long before the hour at which they were expected James rolled himself to the window to wait for their coming. Now that the leaves were off the trees he could just see the car stop at the end of the street and he watched eagerly for the flock of young people to run toward the house. It seemed an interminable wait, yet the car on which they had promised to come was not a minute late when at last it halted and its eager passengers stepped off. James could see the Ethels leading the procession, waving their hands toward the window at which they knew he must be, although they could not see him until they came much nearer.

Dorothy followed them not far behind, and Roger and Helen brought up the rear. Every one of them was laden with parcels of the strangest shapes.

"I know the conductor thought we were Santa Claus's own children," laughed Ethel Blue as they all shook hands with the invalid and inquired after his leg.

"We've come up to have a pasting bee," said Helen, "and we all have ideas for you to carry out."

"So have we," cried a new voice at the door, and Della and Tom came in, also laden with parcels and also bubbling with pleasure at seeing James so well again.

"We shall need quantities of smallish presents that you can manage here at your table just splendidly," explained Ethel Brown.

"And dozens of wrappings of various kinds that you can make, too."

"Great and glorious," beamed James. "'Lay on, Macduff.' I'll absorb every piece of information you give me, like a wet sponge."

"Let's do things in shipshape fashion," directed Roger. "What do you say to boxes first? We'll lay out here our patterns, and materials."

"Let's make one apiece of everything," cried Dorothy, "and leave them all for James to copy."

"And we can open the other bundles afterwards," said Della, "then those materials won't get mixed up with the box materials."

"Save the papers and strings," advised Ethel Brown. "We're going to need a fearful amount of both when wrapping time comes."

"The secretary has had a letter from Mademoiselle," Helen informed the invalid.

"Where from?" James was aflame with interest.

"She's in Belgium; you know she said she was going to try to be sent there. She doesn't mention the name of the town, but she's near enough to the front for wounded to be brought in from the field."

"And she can hear the artillery booming all the time," contributed Ethel Blue.

"And one day she went out right on to the firing line to give first aid."

"Think of that! Our little teacher!"

"She wasn't given those black eyes for nothing! She's game right through!" laughed Helen.

CHAPTER XIII

PASTING

"SOME of these ideas will be more appropriate for Christmas gifts here in America than for our war orphans, it seems to me," said Helen, "but we may as well make a lot of everything because we'll be doing some Christmas work as a club and nothing will be lost."

"Tell me what they are and I can do them last," said James.

"And we can put them on a shelf in the club attic as models," suggested Dorothy.

"Here's an example," said Helen, taking up a pasteboard cylinder. "This is a mailing tube—you know those mailing tubes that you can buy all made, of different sizes. We've brought down a lot of them to-day. Take this fat one, for instance, and cut it off about three inches down. Then cover it with chintz or cretonne or flowered paper or holly paper."

"Line it with the paper, too, I should say," commented James, picking up the pieces that Helen cut off.

"Yes, indeed. Cover two round pieces and fit one of them into the bottom and fasten the other on for a cover with a ribbon hinge, and there you have a box for string, or rubber bands for somebody's desk."

"O.K. for rubber bands," agreed Roger, "but for string it would be better to make a hole in the cover and let the cord run up through."

String Box made from a Mailing Tube String Box made from a Mailing Tube

"How would you keep the cover from flopping up and down when you pulled the string?"

"Here's one very simple way. You know those fasteners that stationers sell to keep papers together? They have a brass head and two legs and when you've pushed the legs through the papers you press them apart and they can't pull out. One of those will do very well as a knob to go on the box part, and a loop of gold or silver cord or of ribbon can be pasted or tied on to the cover."

"If you didn't care whether it was ever used again you could put in the ball of twine with its end sticking through and then paste a band of paper around the joining of the top and the box. It would be pretty as long as the twine lasted."

"It would be a simple matter for the person who became its proud possessor to paste on another strip of paper when he had put in his new ball of twine."

"Any way you fix it," went on Helen, "there you have the general method of making round boxes from these mailing tubes."

"And you can use round boxes for a dozen purposes," said Margaret; "for candy and all the goodies we're going to send the orphans."

"Are you sure they'll keep?" asked careful James.

"Ethel Brown asked the domestic science teacher at school about that, and she's going to give her receipts for cookies and candies that will last at least six weeks. That will be long enough for the Christmas Ship to go over and to make the rounds of the ports where it is to distribute presents."

"Of course we'll make the eatables at the last minute," said Dorothy, "and we'll pack them so as to keep the air out as much as possible."

"Give that flour paste a good boiling," Helen called after Margaret as she left the room to prepare it.

"And don't forget the oil of cloves to keep it sweet," added Ethel Blue.

"These round boxes will be especially good for the cookies," said Ethel Brown, "though the string box would have to go to Father. A string box isn't especially suitable for an orphan."

"If you split these mailing tubes lengthwise and line them inside you get some pretty shapes," went on Helen.

"Rather shallow," commented Della.

"If you split them just in halves they are, but you don't have to do that. Split them a little above the middle and then the cover will be shallower than the box part."

"Right-o," nodded Roger.

"Then you line them and arrange the fastening and hinges just as you described for the string box?" asked James.

"Exactly the same. Another way of fastening them is by making little chintz straps and putting glove snappers on them."

"I don't see why you couldn't put ribbons into both cover and box part and tie them together."

"You could."

"You can use these split open ones for a manicure set or a brush and comb box for travelling."

"Or a handkerchief box."

"If you get tubes of different sizes and used military hair brushes you could make a box for a man, with a cover that slipped over for a long way," said Ethel Blue. "It would be just like the leather ones."

"You make one of those for Uncle Richard for Christmas," advised Ethel Brown. "I rather think the orphans aren't keen on military brushes."

"Oh, I'm just talking out any ideas that come along. As Helen suggested, an idea is always useful some time or other even if it won't do for to-day's orphans."

"I saw a dandy box the other day that we might have put into Mademoiselle's kit," said Roger. "It's a good thing to remember for some other traveller."

"Describe," commanded James.

"I don't think these round boxes would be as convenient for it as a square or oblong one. It had a ball of string and a tube of paste and a pair of small scissors, and tags of different sizes and rubber bands and labels with gum on the back."

"That's great for a desk top," said Della. "I believe I'll make one for Father for his birthday," and she nodded toward Tom who nodded back approvingly.

"A big blotter case is another desk gift. The back is of very stiff cardboard and the corners are of chintz or leather. The blotters are slipped under the corners and are kept flat by them," continued Roger, who had noticed them because of their leather corners.

"A lot of small blotters tied together are easy to put up," contributed Dorothy. "You can have twelve, if you want to, and paste a calendar for a month on to each one."

"I think we ought to make those plain boxes the boys have made for the dresses a little prettier. Can't we ornament them in some way?" asked Ethel Blue.

"The made-over ones are all covered with fancy paper you remember," said Tom.

"I was thinking of the plain ones that are 'neat but not gaudy.' How can we make them 'gaudy'?"

"Christmas seals are about as easy a decoration as you can get," Tom suggested.

"Pretty, too. Those small seals, you mean, that you put on letters. A Santa Claus or a Christmas tree or a poinsettia would look pretty on the smaller sized boxes."

"It would take a lot of them to show much on the larger ones, and that would make them rather expensive. Can't we think up something cheaper?" asked the treasurer.

"I'm daffy over wall paper," cried Dorothy. "I went with Mother to pick out some for one of our rooms the other day and the man showed us such beauties—they were like paintings."

"And cost like paintings, too," growled James feelingly.

"Some of them did," admitted Dorothy. "But I asked him if he didn't have remnants sometimes. He laughed and said they didn't call them remnants but he said they did have torn pieces and for ten cents he gave me a regular armful. Just look at these beauties."

She held up for the others' inspection some pieces of paper with lovely flower designs upon them.

"But those bits aren't big enough to cover a big box and the patterns are too large to show except on a big box," objected Margaret who had come back with the paste.

"Here's where they're just the thing for decoration of the plain boxes. Cut out this perfectly darling wistaria—so. Could you find anything more graceful than that? You'd have to be an artist to do anything so good. Paste that sweeping, drooping vine with its lovely cluster of blossoms on to the top of one of the largest boxes and that's plenty of decoration."

Dorothy waved her vine in one hand and her scissors in the other and the rest became infected with her enthusiasm, for the scraps of paper that she had brought were exquisite in themselves and admirable for the purpose she suggested.

"Good for Dorothy!" hurrahed James. "Anybody else got any ideas on this decoration need?"

"Paste that vine on to the top of one of the largest boxes" "Paste that vine on to the top of one of the largest boxes"

"I have," came meekly from Ethel Brown. "It isn't very novel but it will work, and it will save money and it's easy."

"Trot her forth," commanded Roger.

"It's silhouettes."

Silence greeted this suggestion.

"They're not awfully easy to do," said Helen doubtfully.

"Not when you make them out of black paper, and you have to draw on the pattern or trace it on and you can hardly see the lines and you get all fussed up over it," acknowledged Ethel. "I've tried that way and I almost came to the conclusion that it wasn't worth the trouble I put into it unless you happened to be a person who can cut them right out without drawing them first."

"I saw a man do that at a bazar once," said Della. "It was wonderful. He illustrated Cinderella. He cut out a coach and tiny horses and the old fairy without drawing anything at all beforehand."

"Nothing doing here," Tom pushed away an imaginary offer of scissors and black paper.

"Here's where my grand idea comes in," insisted Ethel Brown. "My idea is to cut out of the magazines any figures that please you."

"Figures with action would be fun," suggested Roger.

"They'd be prettiest, too. You'll find them in the advertising pages as well as in the stories. Paste them on to your box or whatever you want to decorate, and then go over them with black oil paint."

"Good for old Ethel Brown!" applauded her brother. "I didn't think you had it in you, child! Have you ever tried it?"

"Yes, sir, I have. I knew I'd probably meet with objections from an unimaginative person like you, so I decorated this cover and brought it along as a sample."

It proved to be an idea as dashing as it was simple. Ethel Brown had selected a girl rolling a hoop. A dog, cut from another page, was bounding beside her. Some delicate foliage at one side hinted at a landscape.

"Wasn't it hard not to let the black run over the edges of the picture?" asked Della.

"Yes, you have to keep your wits about you all the time. But then you have to do that any way if you want what you're making to amount to anything, so that doesn't count."

"That's a capital addition, that suggestion of ground that you made with a whisk or two of the brush."

"Just a few lines seem to give the child something to stand on."

"These plans for decoration look especially good to me," said practical James, "because there's nothing to stick up on them. They'll pack easily and that's what we must have for our purpose."

"That's true," agreed Helen. "For doing up presents that don't have to travel it's pretty to cut petals of red poinsettia and twist them with wire and make a flower that you can tuck in under the string that you tie the parcel with—"

"Or a bit of holly. Holly is easily made out of green crêpe paper or tissue paper," cried Della.

"But as James says, none of the boxes for the orphans can have stick-ups or they'll look like mashed potatoes when they reach the other side."

"We'll stow away the poinsettia idea for home presents then," said Margaret. "What we want from James, however, is a lot of boxes of any and every size that he can squeeze out."

"No scraps thrown away, old man," decreed Tom, "for even a cube of an inch each way will hold a few sweeties."

"Orders received and committed to memory," acknowledged the invalid, saluting.

"By the way, I learned an awfully interesting thing to-day," said Helen.

"Name it," commanded Roger, busy with knife and pastepot making one of the twine and tag boxes that he had described.

"I'll tell you while we each make one of the things we've been talking about so that we can leave them for patterns with James."

Dorothy had already set about applying her wistaria vine to the cover of a box whose body Tom was putting together. Ethel Blue was making a string box from a mailing tube, covering it with a scrap of chintz with a very small design; Ethel Brown was hunting in an old magazine for figures suitable for making silhouettes; James was writing in a notebook the various hints that had been bestowed upon him so generously that he feared his memory would not hold them all without help; Helen and Della were measuring and cutting some cotton cloth that was to be used in the gifts that Della was eager to tell about.

"By the time Helen has told her tale I'll be ready to explain my gift idea," she said.

"Go on, then, Helen," urged James, "I'm ready to 'start something' myself, in a minute."

"You and Margaret have heard us talk about our German teacher?"

"We've seen her," said Margaret. "She was at our entertainment."

"So she was. I remember, she and her mother sat right behind the old ladies from the Home."

"And they knitted for the soldiers whenever the lights were up."

"I guess Mrs. Hindenburg knitted when the lights were off, too," said Helen. "I've seen her knitting with her eyes shut."

"She sent in some more wristers for the orphans the other day," said Dorothy. "She has made seven pairs so far, and three scarfs and two little sweaters."

"Some knitter," announced Roger.

"Fräulein knits all the time, too, but she says she can't keep up with her mother. This is what I wanted to tell you—you remember when Roger first went there she told him that Fräulein's betrothed was in the German army. Well, yesterday she told us who he is."

"Is it all right for you to tell us?" warned Roger.

"It's no secret. She said that the engagement was to have been announced as soon as he got back from Germany and that many people knew it already."

"Is he an American German?"

"It's our own Mr. Schuler."

Roger gave a whistle of surprise; the Ethels cried out in wonder, and the Hancocks and the Watkinses who did not know many Rosemont people, waited for the explanation.

"Mr. Schuler was the singing teacher in the high school year before last and last year," explained Helen. "Last spring he had to go back to Germany in May so he was there when the army was mobilized and went right to the front."

"It does come near home when you actually know a soldier fighting in the German army and a nurse in a hospital on the Allies' side," said Roger thoughtfully.

"It makes it a lot more exciting to know who Fräulein's betrothed is."

"Does she speak of him?" asked Margaret.

"She talked about him very freely yesterday after her mother mentioned his name."

"I suppose she didn't want the high school kids gossiping about him," observed Roger.

"As we are," interposed James.

"We aren't gossiping," defended Helen. "She looks on the Club members as her special friends—she said so. She knows we wouldn't go round at school making a nine days' wonder of it. She knows we're fond of her."

"We are," agreed Roger. "She's a corker. I wonder we didn't think of its being Mr. Schuler."

"Her mother always mentioned him as 'my daughter's betrothed'; and Fräulein yesterday kept saying 'my betrothed.' We might have gone on in ignorance for a long time if Mrs. Hindenburg hadn't let it slip out yesterday."

"Well, I hope he'll come through with all his legs and arms uninjured," said Roger. "I hope it for Fräulein's sake, and for his, too. He's a bully singing teacher."

"Has she heard from him since the war began?"

"Several times, but not for a month now, and she's about crazy with anxiety. He was in Belgium when he got the last letter through and of course that means that he has been in the very thick of it all."

"Poor Fräulein!" sighed Ethel Blue, and the others nodded seriously over their work.

CHAPTER XIV

JAMES'S AFTERNOON PARTY

"NOW are you ready to take in all the difficulties of my art object?" asked Della.

"Trot her out," implored James.

"It's picture books."

A distinct sniff went over the assembly, only kept in check by a desire to be polite.

"There can't be anything awfully new about picture books," said Tom.

"Especially cloth picture books. You and Helen have been cutting out cambric for cloth picture books," accused Ethel Brown.

"Della has been making some variations, though." Helen came to Della's rescue. "She's made some with the leaves all one color, pink or blue; and here's another one with a variety—two pages light pink, and the next two pages pale green."

Ethel Brown cast a more interested eye toward the picture book display.

"How do you sew them together?" she asked.

"You can do it on the machine and let it go at that. In fact, that's the best plan even if you go on to add some decoration of feather-stitching or cat-stitching. The machine stitching makes it firmer."

"Is there an interlining?"

"I tried them with and without an interlining. I don't think an interlining is necessary. The two thicknesses of cambric are all you need."

"Dicky has a cloth book with just one thickness for each page," said Ethel Brown.

"But that's made of very heavy cotton," explained Helen.

"You cut your cambric like a sheet of note-paper," said Della.

"Haven't my lessons on scientific management soaked in better than that?" demanded Roger. "If you want to save time you cut just as many sheets of note-paper, so to speak, as your scissors will go through."

"Certainly," retorted Della with dignity. "I took it for granted that the members of the U. S. C. had learned that. Put two sheets of this cambric note-paper together flat and stitch them. That makes four pages to paste on, you see. You can make your book any size you want to and have just as many pages as you need to tell your story on."

"Story? What story?" asked Ethel Blue, interestedly.

"Aha! I thought you'd wake up!" laughed Della. "Here, my children, is where my book differs from most of the cloth picture books that you ever saw. My books aren't careless collections of pictures, with no relation to each other. Here's a cat book, for instance. Not just every-day cats, though I've put in lots of cats and some kodaks of my own cat. There are pictures of the big cats—lions and tigers—and I've put in some scenery so that the child who gets this book will have an idea of what sort of country the beasts really live in."

"It's a natural history book," declared James.

"Partly. But it winds up with 'The True Story of Thomas's Nine Lives.'"

"The kid it is going to won't know English," objected Roger.

"Oh, I haven't written it out. It's just told in pictures with , , , through at the head of each page. They'll understand."

"Do you see what an opportunity the different colored cambric gives?" said Helen. "Sometimes Della uses colored pictures or she paints them, and then she makes the background harmonize with the coloring of the figures."

"Why couldn't you make a whole book of my silhouettes?" demanded Ethel Brown.

"Bully!" commended James.

"You can work out all sorts of topics in these books, you see," Della went on. "There are all the fairy stories to illustrate and 'Red Riding Hood,' and the 'Bears,' and when you get tired of making those you can have one about 'The Wonders of America,' and put in Niagara."

"And the Rocky Mountains," said Tom.

"And the Woolworth Building," suggested Ethel Brown.

"And a cotton field with the negroes picking cotton," added Ethel Blue.

"There wouldn't be any trouble getting material for that one," said Helen.

"Nor for one on any American city. I've got one started that is going to show New York from the statue of Liberty to the Jumel Mansion and the Van Cortland House, with a lot of other historical buildings and skyscrapers and museums in between."

"We'll be promoting emigration from the old country after the war is over if we show the youngsters all the attractions that Uncle Sam has to offer."

"There'll be a lot of them come over anyway so they might as well learn what they'll see when they arrive."

"I see heaps of opportunities in that idea," said Roger. "There's a chance to teach the kiddies something by these books if we're careful to be truthful in the pictures we put in."

"Not to make monkeys swinging down the forests of Broadway, eh?" laughed Tom.

"If I'm to do a million or two of these you'll all have to help me get the pictures together," begged James.

"I've brought some with me you can have for a starter," said Della, "and I'm collecting others and keeping them in separate envelopes—animals in one and buildings in another and so on. It will make it easier for you."

"Muchas gracias, Señorita," bowed James, who was just beginning Spanish and liked to air a "Thank you" occasionally.

"I know what I'm going to make for some member of my family," declared Roger.

"Name it, it will be such a surprise when it comes."

"Probably it will go to Grandmother Emerson so I don't mind telling you that I think I'll write a history of our summer at Chautauqua and illustrate it."

"That's the best notion that ever came from Roger," approved James. "I think I'll make one and give it to Father. The Recognition Day procession and all that, you know."

"Envelopes make me think that we may have some small gifts—cards or handkerchiefs—that we can send in envelopes," said Ethel Blue, "and we ought to decorate them just as much as our boxes."

"They won't be hard. Any of the ideas we've suggested for the boxes will do—flowers and silhouettes, and seals. You're a smarty with watercolors so you can paint some original figures or a tiny landscape, but the rest of us will have to keep to the pastepot," laughed Margaret.

"For home gifts we can write rhymes to put into the envelopes, but I suppose it wouldn't do for these European kids," said Tom. "We don't know where they're going, you see, and it would never do if an English child got a German rhyme or the other way round."

"O-oh, ne-ver," gasped Ethel Blue whose quick imagination sympathized with the feelings of a child to whom such a thing happened. "We'll have to make them understand through their eyes."

"Fortunately Santa Claus with his pack speaks a language they can all understand," nodded Roger.

"Here comes his humble servant right now," exclaimed Mrs. Hancock at the door.

Tom ran to hold it open for her, and Roger relieved her of the waiter which she was carrying.

"James has to have an egg-nog at this time," she explained, "so I thought all of you might like to be 'picked up' after your hard afternoon's work."

These sentiments were greeted with applause though Tom insisted that the best part of the afternoon was yet to come as he had not yet had a chance to tell about his invention.

"One that you'll appreciate tremendously, Mrs. Hancock," he said gravely. "All housekeepers will. You must get Margaret to make you one."

"Don't tell her what it is and I can give it to her for Christmas," cried Margaret.

James's egg-nog and his wafers were placed on the table beside him. The others sat at small tables, of which there were several around the room, and drank their egg-nog and ate their cakes with great satisfaction.

"Tell me how this egg-nog is made," begged Helen. "It is delicious and I'm sure Mother would like to know."

"Mother always has it made the same way," replied Margaret. "I'm sure it is concocted out of six eggs and half a pound of sugar, and three pints of whipped cream and a dash of cinnamon and nutmeg."

"It's so foamy—that isn't the whipped cream alone."

"First you beat the yolks of the eggs and the sugar together until it is all frothy. Then you beat the whites of the eggs by themselves until they are stiff and you stir that in gently. Then you put the spice on top of that and lastly you heap the whipped cream on top of the whole thing."

"It's perfectly delicious," exclaimed Dorothy, "and so is the fruit cake."

"Mother prides herself on her fruit cake. It is good, isn't it? She's going to let me make some to send to the orphans."

"Won't that be great. Baked in ducky little pans like these."

"They'll keep perfectly, of course."

"Would your mother let us have the receipt now so we could be practicing it to make some too?" asked Dorothy.

"I'm sure she'd be delighted," and Margaret ran off to get her mother's manuscript cook book from which Dorothy copied the following receipt:

"Fruit Cake

"½ cup butter

¾ cup brown sugar

¾ cup raisins, chopped

¾ cup currants

½ cup citron, cut in small pieces

½ cup molasses

eggs

½ cup milk

cups flour

½ teaspoon soda

teaspoon cinnamon

½ teaspoon allspice

¼ teaspoon nutmeg

¼ teaspoon cloves

½ teaspoon lemon extract or vanilla

"Sift the flour, soda and spices together. Beat the eggs, add the milk to them. Cream the butter, add the sugar gradually, add the molasses, the milk and egg, then the flour gradually. Mix the fruit, sift a little flour over it, rub it in the flour, add to it the mixture. Add the extract. Stir and beat well. Fill greased pans two-thirds full. Bake in a moderately hot oven one and a quarter hours if in a loaf. In small sizes bake slowly twenty to thirty minutes."

"I'm ready to hear what Tom's got to offer," said James, leaning back luxuriously in his chair after the remains of the feast had been taken away.

"Mine is a paper-cutting scheme," responded Tom. "Perhaps it won't come easy to everybody, but on a small scale I'm something of a paper cutter myself."

"Dull edged?" queried Roger.

"Hm," acknowledged Tom. "I can't illustrate 'Cinderella' like the man Della saw, but I can cut simple figures and I want to propose one arrangement of them to this august body."

"Fire ahead," came Roger's permission.

"It's just a variation of the strings of paper dolls that I used to make for Della when she was a year or two younger than she is now."

Della received this taunt with a puckered face.

"Fold strips of paper and then cut one figure of a little girl" "Fold strips of paper and then cut one figure of a little girl"

"You fold strips of white paper—or blue or yellow or any old color—in halves and then in halves again and then again, until it is about three inches wide. Then you cut one figure of a little girl, letting the tips of the hands and skirts remain uncut. When you unfold the strip you have a string of cutey little girls joining hands. See?"

They all laughed for all of them had cut just such figures when they were children.

"Now my application of this simple device," went on Tom in the solemn tones of a professor, "is to make them serve as lamp shades."

"For the orphans?" laughed Roger.

"For the orphans I'm going to cut about a bushel of strips of all colors. Children always like to play with them just so."

"I don't see why those of us who can't draw couldn't cut a child or a dog or some figure from a magazine and lay it on the folded paper and trace around the edges and then cut it," suggested Dorothy.

A String of Paper Dolls A String of Paper Dolls

"You could perfectly well. All you have to remember is to leave a folded edge at the side, top and bottom. You can make a row of dogs standing on their hind paws and holding hands—forepaws—and the ground they are standing on will fasten them together at the bottom."

"How does the lamp shade idea work out?" asked Helen with Grandfather Emerson's Christmas gift in mind.

"You cut a string of figures that are fairly straight up and down, like Greek maidens or some conventional vases or a dance of clowns. Then you must be sure that your strip is long enough to go around your shade. Then you line it with asbestos paper—the kind that comes in a sort of book for the kitchen."

"I see. You paste the strip right on to the asbestos paper and cut out the figures," guessed James.

"Exactly," replied Tom. "After which you paste the ends of the strip together and there you have your shade ready to slip on to the glass."

Photograph Frame—front Photograph Frame—front

"What keeps it from falling down and off?"

"The shape of the shade usually holds it up. If it isn't the right shape, though, you can run a cord through your figures' hands and tighten them up as much as you need to."

"I think that's a rather jolly stunt of Tom's," commended Roger patronizingly. Tom gave him a kick under the table and James growled a request not to hit his game leg.

Photograph Frame—back Photograph Frame—back

"If you boys are beginning to quarrel it's time we adjourned," decided the president. "Has anybody any more ideas to get off her alleged mind this afternoon?"

"I thought of picture frames," offered James.

"While my hand is in with pasting I believe I'll make some frames—a solid pasteboard back and the front with an oval or an oblong or a square cut out of it. You paste the front on to the back at the edges except at the bottom. You leave that open to put the picture in."

"You can cover that with chintz—cotton, cotton, cotton," chanted Dorothy, who seldom missed a chance to promote the cotton crusade.

"How do you hang it up?" asked Margaret.

"Stick on a little brass ring with a bit of tape. Or you can make it stand by putting a stiff bit of cardboard behind it with a tape hinge."

"That would be a good home present," said Ethel Brown.

"Perfectly good for family photographs. You can make them hold two or three. But you can fix them up for the European kids and put in any sort of picture—a dog or a cat or George Washington or some really beautiful picture."

"I believe in giving them pictures of America or American objects or places or people," said Dorothy.

"Dorothy is the champion patriot of the United Service Club," laughed Roger. "Come on, infants; we must let James rest or Mrs. Hancock won't invite us to come again. I wish you could get over to Rosemont for the movies next week," he added.

"What movies?"

"The churches have clubbed together and hired the school hall and they're going to get the latest moving pictures from the war zone that they can find. It is the first time Rosemont has ever had the real thing."

CHAPTER XV

PREVENTION

THE Mortons were gathered about the fire in the half hour of the day which they especially enjoyed. Mrs. Morton made a point of being at home herself for this time, and she liked to have all the young people meet her in the dusk and tell her of the day's work and play. It was a time when every one was glad to rest for a few minutes after dressing for dinner.

"I'm sure to get my hair mussed up if I do anything but talk to Mother after I brush it for dinner," Roger was in the habit of explaining, "so it suits me just to stare at the fire."

He was sitting now on the floor beside her with his head leaning against the arm of her chair. Dicky was occupying the Morris chair with her, and the three girls were in comfortable positions, the Ethels on the sofa and Helen knitting a scarf as she sat on a footstool before the blaze.

"You're not trying your eyes knitting in this imperfect light?" asked her mother.

"This is plain sailing, Mother. I can rush along on this straight piece almost as fast as Mrs. Hindenburg, and I don't have to look on at all unless a horrid fear seizes me that I've skipped a stitch."

"Which I hope you haven't done."

"Never really but there have been several false alarms."

"How is Fräulein?"

"All right, I guess."

"Did you see her to-day?"

"We had German compo to-day. I didn't do much with it."

"Why not?"

"It didn't seem to go off well. I don't know why. Perhaps I didn't try as hard as usual."

"Did it disturb Fräulein?"

"Did what disturb Fräulein?"

"That you didn't do your lesson well."

"Disturb Fräulein? I don't know. Why should it disturb her? I should think I was the one to be disturbed."

"Were you?"

"Was I disturbed? Well, no, Mother, to tell the truth I didn't care much. That old German is so hard and the words all break up so foolishly—somehow it didn't seem very important to me this morning. And Fanny Shrewsbury said something awfully funny about it under her breath and we got laughing and—no, I wasn't especially disturbed."

"Although you had a poor lesson and didn't try to make up for it by paying strict attention in the class!"

"Why, Mother, I, er—"

Helen stopped knitting.

"You think I'm taking too seriously a poor lesson that wasn't very bad, after all? Possibly I am, but I've been noticing that all of you are more careless lately than I want my girls and boys to be."

Mrs. Morton stroked Roger's hair and looked around at the handsome young faces illuminated by the firelight.

"You mean us, too?" cried the Ethels, sitting up straight upon the sofa.

"You, too."

"We haven't meant to be careless, Mother," said Roger soberly. His mother's good opinion was something he was proud of keeping and she was so fair in her judgments that he felt that he must meet any accusations like the present in the honest spirit in which they were made.

"Do you want to know what I think is the trouble with all of you?"

Every one of them cried out for information, even Dicky, whose "Yeth" rang out above the others.

"If you ask for my candid opinion," responded Mrs. Morton, "I think you are giving so much time and attention to the work of the U. S. C. that you aren't paying proper attention to the small matters of every day life that we must all meet."

"Oh, but, Mother, you approve of the U. S. C."

"Certainly I approve of it. I think it is fine in every way; but I don't believe in your becoming so absorbed in it that you forget your daily duties. Aunt Louise had to telephone to Roger to go over and start her furnace for her yesterday when the sharp snap came, and the Ethels have been rushing off in the morning without doing the small things to help Mary that are a part of their day's work."

"Oh, Mother, they're such little things! She can do them easily once in a while."

"Any one of your morning tasks is a small matter, but when none of them are done they mount up to a good deal for Mary. If there were some real necessity for making an extra bed Mary would do it without complaining, but when, as happened yesterday morning, neither of you Ethels made your bed, and Roger left towels thrown all over his floor, and not one of Helen's bureau drawers was shut tight, and Dicky upset a box of beads and went off to kindergarten without picking them up—don't you see that what meant but a few minutes' work for each one of you meant an hour's work for one person?"

"I'll bet Mary didn't mind," growled Roger.

"Mary is too loyal to say anything, but if your present careless habits should continue we should have to have an extra maid to wait on you, and you know very well that that is impossible."

"I'm sorry, Mother," said Roger penitently. "I'm sorry about the towels and about Aunt Louise and I'm sorry I growled. You're right, of course."

"I rather guess we've been led astray by being so successful with our team work in the club," said Helen thoughtfully. "We've found out that we can do all sorts of things well if we pull together and we've been forgetting to apply co-operation at home."

"Exactly," agreed Mrs. Morton. "And you've been so absorbed in the needs of people several thousand miles away that you overlook the needs of people beside you. What you've been doing to Mary is unkind; what Helen did to Fräulein this morning was unkind."

"Oh, Mother! I wouldn't be unkind to Fräulein for the world."

"I don't believe you would if you thought about it. She certainly is in such sore trouble that she needs all the consideration that her scholars can give her, yet you must have annoyed her greatly this morning."

"I'm afraid Fräulein's used to our not knowing our lessons very well," observed Roger.

"I'm sorry to hear that, but if you know you aren't doing as well as you ought to with your lessons that is the best reason in the world for you to pay the strictest attention while you are in class. Yet Helen says that she and Fanny Shrewsbury were laughing. I'm afraid Fräulein isn't feeling especially content with her work this afternoon."

"Mother, you make me feel like a hound dog," cried Helen. "And I've been talking as if I were so sorry for Fräulein!"

"You are sorry for her as the heroine of a romance, because her betrothed is in the army and she doesn't know where he is or whether he is alive. It sounds like a story in a book. But when you think what that would mean if it were you that had to endure the suffering it wouldn't seem romantic. Suppose Father were fighting in Mexico and we hadn't heard from him for a month—do you think you could throw off your anxiety for a minute? Don't you think you'd have to be careful every instant in school to control yourself? Don't you think it would be pretty hard if some one in school constantly did things that irritated you—didn't know her lessons and then laughed and giggled all through the recitation hour?"

Helen's and Roger's heads were bent.

"Imagine," Mrs. Morton went on, "how you would feel every day when you came home, wondering all the way whether a letter had come; wondering whether, if one had come, it would be from Father or from some one else saying that Father was—wounded."

"Oh, Mother, I can't—" Helen was almost crying.

"You can't bear to think of it; yet—"

"Yet Fräulein was just so anxious and—"

"And we made things worse for her!"

"I know you didn't think—"

"We ought to think. I've excused myself all my life by saying 'I didn't think.' I ought to think."

"'I didn't think' explains, but it doesn't excuse."

"Nothing excuses meanness."

"That's true."

"And it's almost as mean not to see when people are in trouble as it is to see it and not to care."

"I'm glad you're teaching us to be observant, Aunt Marion," said Ethel Blue quietly. "I used to think it was sort of distinguished to be absent-minded and not to pay attention to people, but now I think it's just stupidity."

"Mother," said Roger, sitting up straight, "I've been a beast. Poor Fräulein is worrying herself to pieces every minute of the day and I never thought anything about it. And I let Aunt Louise freeze yesterday morning and Dorothy had to go to school before the house was warmed up and she had a cold to-day because she got chilled. I see your point, and I'm a reformed pirate from this minute!"

Roger rose and squared his shoulders and walked about the room.

"When you think it out it's little things that are hard to manage all the time," he went on thoughtfully. "Here are these little things that we've been pestering Mary about, and when we kids squabble it's almost always about some trifle."

"A pin prick is often more trying than a severe wound," agreed his mother. "You brace yourself to bear a real hurt, but it doesn't seem worth while for a trifle and so you whine about it before you think. If Father and Uncle Richard really were in action all of us would do our best to be brave about it and to bear our trouble uncomplainingly—"

"The way Fräulein does," murmured Helen.

"That's the way when you have a sickness," said Ethel Brown. "When I had the measles you and Mary said I didn't make much fuss, but every time I catch cold I'm afraid all of you hear about it."

"We do," agreed Roger cheerfully.

"I should say, then," remarked Mrs. Morton as Mary appeared at the door to announce dinner, "that this club should bear in mind that it is to serve not only those at a distance but those near home, and not only to serve people in deepest trouble but to serve by preventing suffering."

"I get you, Mother dear," said Roger, taking his father's seat.

"Prevention is a great modern principle that we don't think enough about," said Mrs. Morton.

"I know what you mean—fire prevention," exclaimed Ethel Blue. "Tom Watkins was telling us the other day about the Fire Prevention parade they had in New York. There were a lot of engines and hose wagons and ladder wagons and they were all covered with cards telling how much wiser it was to prevent fire than to let it start and then try to put it out."

"Della saw the parade," said Ethel Brown. "She told me there were signs that said 'It's cheaper to put a sprinkler in your factory than to rebuild the factory'; and 'One cigarette in a factory may cost thousands of dollars in repairs.'"

"The doctors have been working to prevent disease," said Roger. "James has often told me what his father is doing to teach people how to avoid being sick."

"All these clean-up campaigns are really for the prevention of illness as much as the making of cleanliness," said Mrs. Morton.

"Everything of that sort educates people, and we can apply the same methods to our own lives," advised Mrs. Morton. "Why can't we have a household campaign to prevent giving Mary unnecessary work and to avoid irritating each other?"

"All that can be worked in as part of the duties of the Service Club," said Ethel Blue.

"Certainly it can. What's the matter, Ethel Brown?"

Ethel Brown was on the point of tears.

"One of the girls at school gave me an order for cookies the other day," she said, "and I didn't do them because we went over to the Hancocks' that afternoon."

"You got your own punishment there," remarked Roger. "If you didn't fill the order you didn't get any pay."

"That wasn't all. She was going to take them to a cousin of hers who was just getting over the mumps. She wanted to surprise her. She was awfully mad because I didn't make them. She said she had depended on them and she didn't have anything to take to her cousin."

"There you see it," exclaimed Mrs. Morton. "It didn't seem much to Ethel Brown not to make two or three dozen cookies, but in the first place she broke her promise, and in the next place she caused real unhappiness to a girl who was depending on them to give pleasure to her sick cousin."

"You've given us a shake-up we won't forget soon, Mother," remarked Roger. "There's one duty I haven't done this week that you haven't mentioned, but I'm pretty sure you know it so I might as well bring it into the light myself and say I'm sorry."

"What is it?" laughed his mother.

"I haven't been over to see Grandfather and Grandmother Emerson for ten days."

"They'll be sorry."

"I was relying on one of the girls going."

"We haven't been," confessed the Ethels.

"Nor I," admitted Helen.

Mrs. Morton looked serious.

"We love to go there," said Ethel Brown, "but we've been so busy."

"Too busy to be kind to the people near at hand, eh?"

The young people looked ruefully at one another.

"Anyway, watch me be attentive to Fräulein," promised Helen.

She was. She and Roger made a point of giving her as little trouble as possible; and of paying her unobtrusive attentions. Roger carried home for her a huge bundle of exercises; the Ethels left some chestnuts at her door when they came back from a hunt on the hillside, and even Dicky wove her a mat at kindergarten of red and white and black paper—the German colors.

The Mortons were all attention to James, too. Every day they remembered to call him up on the telephone and ask him how his box-making was coming on. He had a telephone extension on the table at his elbow and these daily talks cheered him greatly. The others were leaving the making of most of the pasted articles to him, and they were going on with the manufacture of baskets and leather and brass and copper articles and of odds and ends of various kinds.

"Perhaps I'll be able to get up to Dorothy's next Saturday," James phoned to Roger one day, "if Mrs. Smith wouldn't mind the Club meeting downstairs. I suppose the Pater wouldn't let me try to climb to the attic yet."

Mrs. Smith was delighted to make the change for James's benefit, but before the day came he called up Roger one afternoon in great excitement.

"When did you say those church movies were?" he asked.

"To-morrow evening."

"Father says he'll take me over if he doesn't have a hurry call at the last minute."

Roger gave a whoop that resounded along the wire.

"You'll find the whole Club drawn up at the door of the schoolhouse to meet you," he cried. "The Watkinses are coming out from New York. Will Margaret come with you?"

"She and Mother will go over in the trolley."

As Roger had promised, the Club was drawn up in double ranks before the door when Doctor Hancock stopped his machine close to the step. Roger and Tom ran down to make a chair on which to carry James inside, and Helen and Dorothy were ready with the wheel-chair belonging to the old lady at the Home who had been glad to lend it for the evening to the boy whose acquaintance she had made at the Club entertainment.

James was rather embarrassed at being so conspicuous, but all his Rosemont acquaintances came to speak to him and he was quite the hero of the occasion.

The moving pictures were an innovation in Rosemont. There had been various picture shows in empty stores in the town and they had not all been of a character approved by the parents of the school children who went to them in great numbers. The rooms were dark and there was danger of fire and the pictures themselves were not always suitable for young people to see or agreeable for their elders. The result of a conference among some of the townspeople who had the interests of the place at heart was this entertainment which was the first of a series to be given in the school hall on Friday evenings all through the winter. The films were chosen by a sub-committee and it was hoped that they would be so liked that the poor places down town would find it unprofitable to continue.

The program was pleasantly varied. The story of a country boy who went to New York to make his fortune and who found out that, as in the Oriental story, his fortune lay buried in his own dooryard—in this case in the printing office of his own town—was the opener.

That was followed by a remarkable film showing the habits of swallows and by another whereon some of the flowers of Burbank's garden waved softly in the California breeze.

A dramatization of Daudet's famous story called "The Last Class" brought tears to the eyes of the onlookers whose thoughts were much across the Atlantic.

It was a simple, touching tale, and it served appropriately as the forerunner of the war pictures that had just been sent to America by photographers in Germany and France and Belgium.

The first showed troops leaving Berlin, flags flying, bands playing, while the crowds along the street waved a cheerful parting, though once in a while a woman bent her head behind her neighbor's shoulder to hide her tears.

There were scenes in Belgium—houses shattered by the bombs of airmen, huge holes dug by exploding shells; wounded soldiers making their way toward the hospitals, those with bandaged heads and arms helping those whose staggering feet could hardly carry them.

It was a serious crowd that followed every movement that passed on the screen before their eyes. The silence was deep.

Then came a hospital scene. Rows upon rows of beds ran from the front of the picture almost out of sight. Down the space between them came the doctors, instruments in hand, and behind them the nurses, the red crosses gleaming on their arm bands.

A stir went through the onlookers.

"It looks like her."

"I believe it is."

"Don't you think so? The one on the right?"

"It is—it's Mademoiselle Millerand!" cried Roger clearly.

The operator, hearing the noise in front of his booth, and all unconscious that he was showing a friend to these townspeople where the pretty young French teacher had lived for two years, almost stopped turning his machine. So slowly it went that there was no doubt among any who had known her. She followed the physician to the bed nearest the front. There they stopped and the doctor turned to Mademoiselle and asked some question. She was ready with bandages. An orderly slipped his arm under the soldier's pillow and raised his head. His eyes were closed and his face was deathly white. The doctor shook his head. Evidently he would not attempt an operation upon so ill a man. He signed to the attendant to lay the man down and as he did so the people in Rosemont, far, far away from the Belgian hospital, heard a piercing shriek.

"Mein Verlobt! My betrothed!" screamed Fräulein Hindenburg.

"That's Schuler."

"Don't you recognize Schuler?"

"No wonder poor Fräulein screamed!"

Kind hands were helping Fräulein and her mother from the hall. Doctor Hancock went out with them to give a restorative to the young woman and to take them home in his car.

"Didn't he die at that very moment, Herr Doctor?" whispered Fräulein, and the doctor was obliged to confess that it seemed so.

"But we can't be sure," he insisted.

Fräulein's agitation put an end to the entertainment for that evening. Indeed, the film was almost exhausted when the bitter sight came to her. The people filed out seriously.

"If that poor girl has been in doubt about her betrothed, now she knows," one said to another.

"Do you think he really died?" James asked his father as they were driving home.

"I'm afraid he did, son. But there is just a chance that he didn't because the film changed just there to another scene so you couldn't tell."

"That might have been because they didn't want to show a death scene."

"I'm afraid it was."

CHAPTER XVI

FOR SANTA CLAUS'S PACK

JAMES telephoned Dorothy that he was going to be at her house on the afternoon of the Club meeting if it was going to be downstairs and Dorothy replied that her mother was very glad to let them have the dining room to work in. All the members had arrived when Doctor Hancock stopped his car at the door and Margaret got out and rang the bell for Roger's and Tom's help in getting James into the house. Everybody hailed him with pleasure and everybody's tongue began at once to chatter about the dramatic happening of the evening before.

"I'm perfectly crazy to hear everything you've learned this morning," said Margaret, "but before we start talking about it I want to make a beginning on a basket so I can be working while I listen."

"Me, too," said James. "I've pasted enough boxes and gimcracks to fill a young cottage. In fact they are now packed in a young cottage that Father is going to bring over some day when he hasn't any other load. He said the car wouldn't hold it and Margaret and him and me all at the same time this afternoon."

"We've been making all sorts of things this week," said Ethel Brown. "I'm just finishing the last of a dozen balls that I've been covering with crochet. It's the simplest thing in the world and they're fine for little children because the slippery rubber balls slide out of their fingers and these are just rough enough for their tiny paws to cling to."

"I've been making those twin bed-time dolls," said Ethel Blue. "You've seen them in all the shops—just ugly dolls of worsted—but mine are made like the Danish Nisse, the elves that the Danes use to decorate their Yuletide trees."

She held up a handful of wee dolls made of white worsted, doubled until the little figure was about a finger long. A few strands on each side were cut shorter than the rest and stood out as arms. A red thread tied a little way from the top indicated the neck; another about the middle defined the waist; the lower part was divided and each leg was tied at the ankle with red thread, and a red thread bound the wrists. On the head a peaked red hat of flannel or of crochet shaded a face wherein two black stitches represented the eyes, a third the nose, and a red dot the ruby lips. From the back of the neck a crocheted cord about eighteen inches long connected one elf with his twin.

"What's the idea of two?" inquired Tom.

"To keep each other company. You tie them on to a wire of the baby's crib and they won't get lost."

"Or on to the perambulator."

"They don't take long to make—see, I wind the wool over my fingers, so, to get the right length, and then I tie them as quick as a wink; and when I feel in the mood of making the caps I turn off a dozen or two of them—"

"And the cord by the yard, I suppose."

"Just about. I've made quantities of these this week and I'm not going to make any more, so I'll help with the baskets or the stenciling."

"I've been jig-sawing," said Roger. "I've made jumping jacks till you can't rest."

"Where did you get your pattern?" asked Tom who also was a jig sawyer.

Jumping Jack Jumping Jack

"I took an old one of Dicky's that was on the downward road and pulled it to pieces so that I could use each part for a pattern. I cut out ever so many of each section. Then I spent one afternoon painting legs and arms and jackets and caps, and Ethel Blue painted the faces for me. I'm not much on expression except my own, you know."

"Have you put them together yet?"

"Dorothy has been tying the pull strings for me this afternoon and I'm going to do the glueing now while you people are learning baskets."

"James ought to do the glueing for you," suggested Margaret in spite of James's protesting gestures.

Roger laughed.

"I wouldn't be so mean as to ask him," he said. "He's stuck up enough for one lifetime, I suspect."

"I've been jigging, too," confessed Tom.

"Anything pretty?" asked Roger.

"Of course something pretty," defended Helen. "Don't you remember the beauty box he made Margaret?"

"I certainly do. Its delicate openwork surpassed any of my humble efforts."

"It was pretty, wasn't it?" murmured Margaret. "The yellow silk lining showed through."

"What I've been doing lately was the very simplest possible toy for the orphans." Tom disclaimed any fine work. "I've just been cutting circles out of cigar boxes and punching two holes side by side in each one. Then I run a string through the two holes. You slip it over your forefinger of each hand and whirl the disk around the string until it is wound up tight and then by pulling the string you keep the whirligig going indefinitely."

"It doesn't look like much of a toy to me," said Della crushingly.

"May be not, ma'am, but I tried it on Dad and Edward and they played with it for ten minutes apiece. You find yourself pulling it in time to some air you're humming in the back of your head."

"Right-o," agreed James. "I had a tin one once and I played with it from morning till night. I believe the orphans will spend most of their waking hours tweaking those cords."

"I'm glad you think so," said Tom. "Roger was so emphatic I was afraid I'd been wasting my time."

"What's Dorothy been up to this week?" asked James.

"Dorothy couldn't make up her mind whether she wanted most to make bags or model clay candlesticks or dress dolls this week," responded Dorothy, "but she finally decided to dress dolls."

"Where did you get the dolls?"

"Some of them I got with treasury money—they're real dolls, and I made galoptious frocks for them out of scraps from piece-bags."

"Were you patient enough to make all the clothes to take off?" asked Della.

"Every identical garment," replied Dorothy emphatically. "Dolls aren't any fun unless you can dress and undress them. I never cared a rap for a doll with its clothes fastened on."

"Nor I."

"Nor I."

"Nor I."

Every girl in the room agreed with this opinion.

"The rag dolls are the ones I believe the children will like best," said Helen; "that is, if they are at all like American children."

"Isn't it funny—I always liked that terrible looking old rag object of mine better than the prettiest one Father ever sent me," agreed Ethel Blue.

"Every child does," said Margaret.

"Dorothy made some fine ones," complimented Helen.

"Did you draw them or did you get the ones that are already printed on cloth?" asked Della.

"Both. The printed ones are a great deal prettier than mine, but Aunt Marion had a stout piece of cotton cloth—"

A shout arose.

"Cotton cloth! That's enough to interest Dorothy in making anything," laughed Tom.

"Almost," agreed Dorothy good-naturedly. "Any way, I used up the piece of cloth making dolls and cats and dogs. I drew them on the cloth and then stitched them on the machine and, I tell you, I remembered the time when Dicky's stuffed cat had an awful accident and lost almost all his inner thoughts, and I sewed every one of the little beasties twice around."

"What did you stuff them with?"

"Some with cotton."

"Ha, ha!"

"Ha!" retorted Dorothy, "and some with rags, and one with sawdust, but I didn't care for him; he was lumpy."

"I didn't know you could paint well enough to color them," said Roger.

"I can't. I did a few but Ethel Blue did the best one. There was a cat that was so fierce that Aunt Marion's cat growled at it. He was a winner!"

"All the rag dolls were dressed in cotton dresses," explained Ethel Brown.

"Of course."

"But the real dolls were positively scrumptious. There was a bride, and a girl in a khaki sport suit, and a boy in a sailor suit, and a baby. They were regular beauties."

All the time that these descriptions had been given Dorothy and the Mortons had been opening packages of rattan and raffia and laying them out on the dining table. James sat in state at one end, his convalescent leg raised on a chair, and his right hand to the table so that he could handle his materials easily.

"I'm simply perishing to hear about Fräulein," he acknowledged. "Do start me on this basket business, Dorothy, so I can hear about her."

"We don't know such an awful lot," said Dorothy slowly as she counted out the spokes for a small basket. "In fact, we don't know anything at all."

"Misery! And my curiosity has been actually on the boil! How many of those sticks do I need?"

"Let's all do the same basket," suggested Ethel Brown. "Then one lecture by Miss Dorothy Smith will do for all of us."

"Doesn't anybody else know how to make them?"

"Della and I do," replied Ethel Blue. "We're going to work on raffia, but you people might just as well all do one kind of basket. We can use any number of them, you know, so it doesn't make any difference if they are all alike."

"We'll start with a basket that measures three inches across the bottom and is two and a half inches deep," announced Dorothy, who was an expert basket maker. "You'll need eight spokes sixteen inches long and one nine inches long."

There was a general cutting and counting of rattan spokes.

"Are you ready? Take your knife and in four rattans make slits long enough to poke the other four rattans through."

"They're rather fat to get through," complained James.

"Make slits long enough to poke the other rattans through. Sharpen them to a point" "Make slits long enough to poke the other rattans through. Sharpen them to a point"

"You'll need eight spokes sixteen inches long and one nine inches long" "You'll need eight spokes sixteen inches long and one nine inches long"

"Sharpen them to a point. Have you put them through so they make a cross with the arms of even length? Then put the single short piece through on one arm—no, not way through, James; just far enough to catch it."

"That's pretty solid just as it is," commented Tom with his head on one side.

"Nevertheless, you must wrap it with a piece of raffia. Watch me; lay your raffia at the left side of the upright arm and bring it across from left to right. Now pass it under the right hand arm and over the bottom arm and under the left hand arm. Instead of covering the wrapping you've just done you turn back and let your bit of raffia go over the left hand arm."

"This weaving process makes the spokes stand out like wheel spokes" "This weaving process makes the spokes stand out like wheel spokes"

"That binds down the beginning end of the raffia," cried Helen.

"Exactly. That's why you do it. Go under the bottom arm and over the right hand arm behind the top arm."

"Back at the station the train started from," announced Margaret.

"So far you've used your weaver—"

"What's that? The raffia?"

"Yes. So far you've used it merely to fasten the centre firmly. Now you really begin to weave under and over the spokes, round and round."

"I could shoot beans through mine," announced James.

"You haven't pulled your weaver tight as you wove. Push it down hard toward the centre. That's it. See how firm that is? You could hardly get water through that—much less beans or hound puppies, as they say in some parts of North Carolina."

"This weaving process makes the spokes stand out like wheel spokes, doesn't it?"

"That's why they're called spokes. By the time you've been round three times they ought all to be standing apart evenly."

"Please, ma'am, my raffia is giving out," grumbled Tom.

"It's time to use a rattan weaver, then. You used raffia at first because the spokes were so near together. Now you use a fine rattan, finer than your spokes. Wet it first. Then catch it behind a spoke and hold on to it carefully until you come to the second time round or it will slip away from you. You're all right as soon as the second row holds the first row in place."

"My rattan weaver is giving out," said Ethel Brown.

"Take another one and lap it over the end of the one that is on the point of death, then go right ahead. If they're too fat at the ends shave them down a bit where they lap."

"This superb creation of mine is three inches across the middle," announced James.

"It's time to turn up the spokes then. Make up your mind how sharply you want the basket to flare and watch it as you weave, or you'll have it uneven."

"Mine seems to have reached a good height for a small work basket," decided Helen, her head on one side.

"Mine isn't quite so high, but I can seem to see a few choice candies of Ethel Brown's concoction resting happily within its walls," said Tom.

"Let's all make the border. Measure the spokes and cut them just three inches beyond the top of the weaving. You'll have to sharpen their tips a little or else you'll have trouble pushing them down among the weavers."

"I get the idea! You bend them into scallops!"

"Wet them first or there'll be broken fence pickets. When you've soaked them until they're pliable enough bend each spoke over to make a scallop and thrust it down right beside its neighbor spoke between the weavers."

"Mine is more than ever a work basket," said Helen when she had completed the edge. "I shall line it with brown and fit it up with a thimble and threads and needles and a tiny pair of scissors."

"Mine, too," was Ethel Brown's decision.

"My sides turn up too sharply," James thought. "I shall call mine a cover for a small flower pot. Then I shan't have to line it!"

"Here are some of the most easily made mats and baskets in the world," announced Della. "They're made just like the braided rugs you find in farm houses in New England. Mother got some in New Hampshire once before we started going to Chautauqua for the summers."

"I've seen them," said Margaret. "There are yards and yards of rags cut all the same width and sewed together and then they are braided and then the braid is sewed round and round."

"You make raffia mats or baskets in just the same way, only you sew them with raffia," explained Della. "You braid the raffia first and that gives you an opportunity to make pretty color combinations."

"A strand of raffia doesn't last forever. How do you splice it?"

"Splice a thick end alongside of a thin end and go ahead. Try to pick out strands of different lengths for your plaiting or they'll all run out at once and have to be spliced at once and it may make them bunchy if you aren't awfully careful."

The braid for easily made rugs and baskets The braid for easily made rugs and baskets

"I saw a beauty basket once made of corn husks braided in the same way. The inside husks are a delicate color you know, and they were split into narrow widths and plaited into a long rope."

"Where the long leaf pine grows," said Dorothy, "they use pine needles in the same way, only they wrap them around with thread—"

"Cotton thread?"

"Cotton thread—of about the same color."

"You can work sweet grass just so, except that you can wrap that with a piece of itself."

"When you have enough material," went on Della, "you begin the sewing. If you're going to make a round or an oblong mat you decide which right at the beginning and coil the centre accordingly. Then all you have to do is to go ahead. Don't let the stitches show and sew on until the mat is big enough."

"And for a basket I suppose you pile the braids upon each other when you've made the bottom the size you want it."

"Exactly. And you can make the sides flare sharply or slightly just as we made them do with the rattan."

"What's the matter with making baskets of braided crêpe paper?" asked James. "My whole being has been wrapped in paper for a week so it may influence my inventive powers unduly, but I really don't see why it shouldn't work."

"I'm sorry to take you off your perch," remarked Ethel Brown, "but I've seen one."

"O—oh!" wailed James in disappointment. "They were pretty though, weren't they?"

"They were beauties. There was a lovely color combination in the one I saw."

"You could make patriotic ones for Fourth of July—red, white, and blue."

"Or green and red ones for Christmas."

"Or all white for Easter."

"Or pinky ones for May Day."

Just at this moment there came a rush of small feet and Dicky burst into the room.

"Hullo," he exclaimed briefly.

"Hullo," cried a chorus in return.

"I've seen her," said Dicky.

"Who is 'her'?" asked Roger.

"Fräulein."

"Fräulein! Dicky, what have you been doing?"

Helen seized him by the arm and drew him to the side of her chair, while all the other members of the Club laid down their work and listened.

Dicky was somewhat embarrassed at being the object of such undivided attention. He climbed up into Helen's lap.

"I heard you talking at breakfatht about Fräulein and how thomebody perhapth wath dead and perhapth wathn't dead, tho I went and athked her if he wath dead."

"Oh, Dicky!"

Helen buried her face in his bobbed hair, and the rest of the Mortons looked at each other aghast.

"We were wondering if it would be an intrusion to send Fräulein some flowers," explained Helen,—"and—"

"—and here Dicky butts right in!" finished Roger.

"I went to the houthe and I rang the bell," continued Dicky, "and an old lady came to the door."

"Mrs. Hindenburg."

"I thaid 'Ith Mith Fräulein at home?' The old lady thaid 'Yeth.' I walked in and there wath Mith Fräulein in front of the fire. I thaid, 'Ith he dead?'"

"You asked her?"

"Great Scott!"

"Fräulein thaid, 'I don't know, Dicky.' And I thaid, 'Here ith a chethnut I found. You can have it.' And Fräulein thaid, 'Thank you, Dicky,' and I that on her lap and the talked to me a long time about the man that perhapth ith dead, and thometimeth the thaid queer wordth—"

"German," interpreted Margaret under her breath.

"And onthe the cried a little, and—"

"Dicky, Dicky, what have you done!"

"I ain't done anything bad, 'coth when I thaid, 'Now I mutht go,' the old lady thaid, 'Thank you for coming.'"

"She did?"

"Perhaps it did Fräulein good to cry. Poor Fräulein!"

"I'm going again."

"Did she ask you?"

"Of courth the athked me. And I thaid I'd go if the'd wear a white dreth. I don't like a black dreth."

Silence reigned about the table.

"I wish I knew whether he's done harm or good," sighed Helen.

"Good, I should say, or Fräulein's mother wouldn't have asked him to come again," said Ethel Blue.

"At this uncertain moment I think we'd better have some refreshments," said Dorothy.

"I'm certainly in need of something sustaining," groaned Roger.

"Then try these sugar cookies of Ethel Brown's."

"Let me write down right now how she makes them," exclaimed Della, borrowing a pencil from Tom. "This is the kind you're going to make for the orphans, isn't it?"

"Yes, they'll keep a long time, especially if they're wrapped in paraffin paper and put into a tin."

"Recite the rule to me."

"I never can remember rules. Dorothy's got it copied into her cook book. Ask her for it."

"Here you are," said Dorothy who had overheard the conversation, "here on page twenty. And I know you're going to ask for the fudge receipt as soon as you taste Ethel Blue's fudge so you might as well copy that at the same time. It's on the next page."

So Della copied diligently while Dorothy brought in the cookies and fudge in question and Helen and Roger discussed Dicky's performance under their breath.

Here is what Della wrote:

"Sugar Cookies or Sand Tarts

" cup butter

 cups sugar

 eggs

½ cups flour

teaspoons baking powder

Extra whites of eggs

½ cups blanched almonds, chopped.

tablespoons sugar—extra

½ teaspoon cinnamon

"Blanch the almonds by putting them in boiling water, let them stand on the table five minutes, remove a few at a time from the water, rub off the skin and dry them in a towel; then chop them.

"Cream the butter, add the sugar gradually, then the beaten eggs. Sift flour and baking powder together, add to the butter mixture gradually, using a knife to cut it in. Add the nuts. If stiff and dry add a few tablespoons milk to moisten slightly, and mould into a dough with the hands. Roll out portions quite thin, on a floured board, cut out with a cutter, brush with the extra whites, slightly beaten. Mix the cinnamon and the two extra tablespoons sugar together, sprinkle over the cookies. Place on a greased tin, bake about five minutes in a moderately hot oven."

"Fudge

" cups brown or white sugar

cup milk or water

tablespoon butter

squares (inch) chocolate (about ¼ cup grated)

½ teaspoon vanilla

"Mix sugar, milk, butter and chocolate in a saucepan; let it melt slowly; bring to a boil and boil about ten minutes, or until a little forms a soft ball when dropped in a cup of cold water. Add the vanilla, stir a few minutes until slightly thick, turn at once into greased tin plates. Cool and cut into blocks. If it crumbles and is sugary, add half a cup or more hot water, melt, boil again, and try as before. If it should not be hard enough it may be boiled a second time."

CHAPTER XVII

THE CLUB WEAVES, STENCILS AND MODELS CLAY

WHETHER Dicky had done something entirely inexcusable or something wise no one was able to decide, but everybody agreed that at any rate it was pleasanter to think that he had brought poor Fräulein some comfort, and that her mother's thanking him for coming seemed to mean that. They all felt somewhat shocked and queer.

"I move, Madam President," said Tom, "that we don't talk about it any more this afternoon. We don't know and probably we never shall know, and so we might as well get to work again. Did you people realize that time is growing short? The Santa Claus Ship is booked to sail the first week in November."

"We did and do realize it," said Helen. "I'd like to know next about these raffia sofa pillows that Ethel Blue and Della have been making."

"The ones we made are sofa pillows for the orphans' dolls," explained Ethel Blue, "or they can be used for pincushions."

"They make thothe at kindergarten," announced Dicky. "I can make thothe. Mine are paper."

"They're made in just about the same way," said Della. "We made a small cushion with double raffia and wove it under and over on a pasteboard loom."

"How do you make that?"

"Just a piece of heavy pasteboard or a light board or you can take the frame of a smashed slate. You fasten the ends of the threads with pins or tacks or tie them around the bars. First you lay all the threads you want in one direction. That's the warp."

"Warp—I remember. I always have to look it up in the dictionary to see which is warp and which is woof."

"Warp is the thread that goes on first. In a rug or a piece of tapestry it's the plain, ugly thread that holds the beautifully colored threads in place. It's the up and down threads. In raffia you have to be careful to alternate the big ends and small ends so that the weaving will be even."

"What do you do when the warp is ready?"

"Before you begin to weave you must make a solid line across the end so that when you run your first bit of woof across it won't just push right up to the bar of the loom and then ravel out when you cut your product off the loom."

"I get the reason for its existence. I should think you'd make it by tying a string right across the loom knotting it into each strand of warp as you pass by."

"That's exactly what you do; and the ends you can leave flying to join in with the fringe."

"Can we weave now?"

"Go ahead. When you've made the cushion square, if you want it square, go around the three remaining sides and tie a break-water, so to speak, so that the weaving won't ravel out. Trim your fringe even and there's one side of your pillow."

"One side would be enough for a pincushion."

"If you want to make a big sofa cushion—a grown up one—you'll have to make a wide plait of raffia—a four strand or six strand braid—or else you'd never get it done."

"The unbraided would be too delicate. I hate to make things that wear out before you can get used to them about the house."

"You'd have to have a bigger loom for something that size."

"It's no trouble to make. Roger nailed mine together," said Ethel Blue.

"Any one want the dimensions?" asked Roger. "Take two pieces of narrow wood twenty-three inches long, and nail two other pieces of lighter stuff each twenty-five inches long on to their tops at the ends. These bits are raised from the table by the thickness of the first piece of lumber. See?"

Tom and James, who were examining Ethel Blue's loom, nodded.

"Then nail slender uprights, ten inches tall, at each of the four corners and connect them by two other thin sticks twenty-five inches long, running just above your first pair of twenty-fives. Do you get it?"

Again the boys nodded.

"That's all there is to it, and you really don't need to make that for a plain, smooth plank will do at a pinch."

"How do you carry your woof across?" asked Margaret. "Your hand would be in its own way, I should think."

"You thread the raffia into a wooden bodkin about twenty-six inches long."

"I can see that you must draw the cross threads down tight the way we did in weaving the baskets," said James.

"Indeed you must or you'll turn out a sleazy piece of weaving," answered Della.

"There must be oceans of articles you can make out of woven raffia."

"Just about everything that you can make out of a piece of cloth of the same size."

"Of cotton cloth? Ha!"

"Or silk."

"Handkerchief cases and collar cases."

"Coverings for boxes of all kinds. Another material for James to glue on to pasteboard."

"I see lots of chances for it," he answered seriously.

"I believe old James is really taking kindly to pasting," laughed Tom.

"Certainly I am. It's a bully occupation," defended James.

"There are a thousand things that can be made of raffia—you can make lace of it like twine lace, and make articles out of the lace; and you can make baskets of a combination of rattan and raffia, using the raffia for wrapping and for sewing. But we have such a short time left that I think those of us who are going to do any raffia work had better learn how to weave evenly and make pretty little duds out of the woven stuff."

"Wise kid," pronounced Roger. "Now what's little Margaret going to teach us this afternoon?"

"Little Margaret" made a puckered face at this appellation, but she came promptly to the front.

"Ethel Brown and Dorothy have been teaching me to stencil. They could teach the rest of you a great deal better than I can, but they've done their share this afternoon so I'll try."

"Go on," urged Ethel Brown. "We'll help you if you forget."

"If you'll excuse me I'll go to the attic and get my clay," said Dorothy. "I found a new idea for a candlestick in a book this morning and I want to make one before I forget it."

Margaret was in the full swing of explanation when Dorothy returned.

"Why this frown, fair Coz?" demanded Roger in a Shakesperean tone.

"It's the queerest thing—I thought I had enough clay for two pairs of candlesticks and it seems to have shrunk or something so there'll only be one and that mighty small."

"'Mighty small,'" mimicked Roger. "How large is 'mighty small'?"

"Don't bother me, Roger. I'll start this while Margaret talks."

"When a drawing fit seizes Ethel Blue again we'll get her to make us some original stencils," said Helen. "These that we bought at the Chautauqua art store will do well enough for us to learn with."

"They are very pretty," defended Dorothy.

"Mine won't be any better, only they will be original," said Ethel Blue.

"I hate to mention it," said Tom in a whisper, "but I'm not perfectly sure that I know what a stencil is."

There was a shout from around the table.

"Never mind, Thomas," soothed Roger, patting his friend on the shoulder. "Confession is good for the soul. A stencil, my son, is a thin sheet of something—pasteboard, the girls use—with a pattern cut out of it. You lay the stencil down on a piece of cloth or canvas or board or whatever you want to decorate, and you scrub color on all the part of the material that shows through."

"Methinks I see a great light," replied Tom, slapping his forehead. "When you lift the stencil there is your pattern done in color."

Roger and James leaned forward together and patted Tom's brow.

"Such it is to have real intellect!" they murmured in admiring accents.

Tom bowed meekly.

"Enlighten me further—also these smarties. What kind of paint do you use?"

"Tapestry dyes or oil paints. It depends somewhat on your material. If you want to launder it, use the dye."

"Fast color, eh?"

"When you wash it, set the color by soaking your article in cold water salted. Then wash it gently in the suds of white soap. Suds, mind you; don't touch the cake of soap to it."

"I promise you solemnly I'll never touch a cake of soap to any stenciling I do."

"You're ridiculous, Roger. No, I believe you won't!"

"Here's a piece of cloth Ethel Brown is going to make into a doll's skirt. See, she's hemmed it already and I'll put this simple star stencil on the hem. Where's a board, Dorothy?"

Dorothy brought a sewing board and the others watched Margaret pin her material down hard upon it and fasten the stencil over that.

"Good girl! You've got them so tight they won't dare to shiver," declared Tom.

"Do you notice that this stencil has been shellacked so the edges won't roughen when I scrub? Stiff bristle brushes are what I'm using." Margaret called their attention to her utensils. "And I have a different brush for each color. Also I have an old rag to dabble the extra color off on to."

"Are you ready? Go!" commanded Roger.

"I'll put this simple star stencil on the hem" "I'll put this simple star stencil on the hem"

Margaret scrubbed hard and succeeded in getting a variety of shading through the amount of paint that she allowed to soak entirely through or partway through the material. When she had done as many stars as there were openings on the pattern she took out the pins and moved the stencil along so that the holes came over a fresh piece of material, making sure that the space between the first new star and the last old one was the same as that between the stars on the stencil.

"How can we boys apply that?" asked James.

"You can stencil on anything that you would decorate with painting," said Ethel Brown.

"Your jig-saw disks, Tom. Stencil a small conventional pattern on each one—a star or a triangle."

"Here's a stencil of a vine that would be a beauty on one of your large plain pasteboard boxes, James."

"Dorothy has been turning white cheesecloth doll clothes into organdie muslins by stenciling on them these tiny sprays of roses and cornflowers and jasmine."

"I'm going to do roosters and cats and dogs on a lot of bibs for the babies."

"You'd better save a few in case Mademoiselle really sends us that Belgian baby."

"I'll make some more if it does turn up."

"Aunt Marion gave me some cotton flannel—"

"Cot—ton!"

"Cotton flannel, yes, sir; and I've made it into some little blankets for tiny babies. I bound the raw edges, and on some of them I did a cross stitch pattern and on others I stenciled a pattern."

"It saves time, I should say."

"Lots. When you have ever so many articles gathered, just have a stenciling bee and you can turn out the decoration much faster than by doing even a wee bit of embroidery."

"If the Belgian baby really comes, let's make it a play-house. The boys can do the carpentry and we can all make the furniture and I'm wild to stencil some cunning curtains for the windows."

"I'll draw you a fascinating pattern for it."

"There's my candlestick half done," said Dorothy mournfully, "and I can't finish it. I don't understand about that clay."

"Perhaps it dried up and blew away."

"It did dry, but I moistened it and kneaded it and cut it in halves with a wire and put the inside edges outside and generally patticaked it but I'm sure it's not more than a quarter the size it was when I left it in the attic yesterday afternoon."

"You seem to have made a great mess on the floor over there by the window; didn't you slice off some and put it in that cup?"

"That's my 'slip.' It only took a scrap to make that. It's about as thick as cream and you use it to smooth rough places and fill up cracks with. No, that wouldn't account for much of any of the clay."

"How did you make this thing, anyway?" asked James turning it about.

"Careful. I took a saucer and put a wet rag in it and then I made a clay snake and coiled it about the way you make those coiled baskets, only I smoothed the clay so you can't see the coils. I hollowed it on the inside like a saucer. Then I put another wet rag inside my clay saucer and a china saucer inside that and turned them all upside down on my work board, and took off the original china saucer and smoothed down the coils on the underside of the clay saucer."

Tom drew a long breath.

"Take one yourself," he suggested. "You'll need it, you talk so fast."

"It stiffened while Margaret was doing her stenciling. When it was firm enough to handle I turned it over again and took out the small china saucer and smoothed off any marks it had left."

"It's about time to build up the candle holder, isn't it?"

Dorothy's Candlestick Dorothy's Candlestick

"Did you see me bring in a short candle? I wrapped it in a wet rag and stood it exactly in the middle of the clay saucer. Then I roughened the clay around it and wet the rough part with slip and pressed a fresh little snake round the foot of the candle. The slip makes it stick to the roughening, so you have to roughen the top of every coil and moisten it with slip."

"You finished off the top of that part very smoothly," complimented Helen.

"When it's stiff enough you take out the candle and smooth the inside. Here's where I'm stumped. I haven't got enough clay for a handle."

"How do you make the handle?"

"Pat out another snake and make a hoop attached to the holder and another one rolling up on to the lip of the saucer."

"As if the serpent were trying to put his tail into his mouth."

"I shall have to just smooth this over with a soft brush and wrap it up in a wet cloth until I get some more clay. If I let it get hard I can't finish it."

"What's that drip, Dorothy?" asked Helen, as a drop of water fell on the table before her.

They all looked at the ceiling where drops of water were assembling and beginning to fall with a soft splash. There was a scramble to get their work out of the way. Dorothy brought a salad bowl and placed it where it would catch the water and then ran to investigate the cause of the trouble.

At a cry from upstairs Helen and the Ethels ran to her help. Roger went to the foot of the stairs and called up to inquire if they wanted his assistance. Evidently they did, for he, too, disappeared. In a few minutes he re-appeared bearing Dicky in his arms—a Dicky sopping wet and much subdued.

"What in the world?" everybody questioned.

"Dorothy's found her clay," said Roger. "Come on, old man. Wrap Aunt Louise's tweed coat around you—so—and run so you won't catch cold," and the two boys disappeared out of the front door, Dicky stumbling and struggling with the voluminous folds of his aunt's garment.

Dorothy and the other girls came down stairs in a few minutes.

"Do telephone to Aunt Marion's and see if Mother is there and ask her to come home," Dorothy begged Helen, while she gathered cloths and pans and went upstairs again, taking the maid with her.

"What did Dicky do?" asked the others again.

Both Ethels burst into laughter.

"He must have gone up in the attic and found Dorothy's clay, for he had filled up the waste pipe of the bath tub—"

"—and turned on the water, I'll bet!" exclaimed Tom.

"That's just what he did. It looks as if he'd been trying to float about everything he could find in any of the bedrooms."

"Probably he had a glorious time until the tub ran over and he didn't know how to stop it."

"Dicky's a great old man! I judge he didn't float himself!"

"Now Dorothy can finish her candlestick handle!"

CHAPTER XVIII

ETHEL BLUE AWAITS A CABLE

MRS. SMITH begged that the meeting should not adjourn, and under her direction the trouble caused by Dicky's entrance into the navy was soon remedied, although it was evident that the ceiling of the dining-room would need the attention of a professional.

Roger soon returned with the news that the honorary member of the Club had taken no cold, and every one settled down to work again, even Dorothy, who rescued enough clay from Dicky's earthworks to complete the handle of her candlestick.

"I'd like to bring a matter before this meeting," said Tom seriously when they were all assembled and working once more.

"Bring it on," urged the president.

"It isn't a matter belonging to this Club, but if there isn't any one else to do it it seemed to me—and to Father when I spoke to him about it—that we might do some good."

"It sounds mysterious. Let's have it," said James.

"It seemed to me as I thought over those movies the other night that there was a very good chance that that man Schuler—your singing teacher, you know, Fräulein's betrothed—wasn't dead after all."

"It certainly looked like it—the way he fell back against the orderly—he didn't look alive."

"He didn't—that's a fact. At the same time the film made one of those sudden changes right at that instant."

"Father and I thought that was so a death scene shouldn't be shown," said James.

"That's possible, but it's also possible that they thought that was a good dramatic spot to leave that group of people and go off to another group."

"What's your idea? I don't suppose we could find out from the film people."

"Probably not. It would be too roundabout to try to get at their operator in Belgium and very likely he wouldn't remember if they did get in touch with him."

"He must be seeing sights like that all the time."

"Brother Edward suggested when he heard us talking about it that we should send a cable to Mademoiselle and ask her. She must have known Mr. Schuler here in the school at Rosemont."

"Certainly she did."

"Then she would have been interested enough in him to recall what happened when she came across him in the hospital."

"How could we get a message to her? We don't know where that hospital was. They don't tell the names of places even in newspaper messages, you know. They are headed 'From a town near the front.'"

"Here's where Edward had a great idea—that is, Father thought it was workable. See what you think of it."

The Club was growing excited. The Ethels stopped working to listen, Helen's face flushed with interest, and the boys leaned across the table to hear the plan to which Rev. Herbert Watkins had given his approval. They knew that Tom's father, in his work among the poor foreigners in New York, often had to try to hunt up their relatives in Europe so that this would not be a matter of guesswork with him.

"It's pretty much guesswork in this war time," admitted Tom when some one suggested it. "You can merely send a cable and trust to luck that it will land somewhere. Here's Edward's idea. He says that the day we went to see Mademoiselle sail she told him that she was related to Monsieur Millerand, the French Minister of War. It was through her relationship with him that she expected to be sent where she wanted to go—that is, to Belgium."

"She was sent there, so her expectation seems to have had a good foundation."

"That's what makes Edward think that perhaps we can get in touch with her through the same means."

"Through Monsieur Millerand?"

"He suggests that we send a cable addressed to Mademoiselle—"

"Justine—"

"—Millerand in the care of Monsieur Millerand, Minister of War. We could say 'Is Schuler dead?' and sign it with some name she'd know in Rosemont.

She'd understand at once that in some way news of his being in Belgium had reached here."

"It seems awfully uncertain."

"It is uncertain. Even if she got the cable she might not be able to send a reply. Everything is uncertain about it. At the same time if we could get an answer it would be a comfort to Fräulein even if the message said he had died."

"I believe that's so. It's not knowing that's hardest to bear."

"Don't you think Mademoiselle would have sent word to Fräulein if he had died?"

"I don't believe she knew they were engaged. No one knew until after the war had been going on for several weeks. If ever she wrote to any one in Rosemont she might mention having seen him, but I don't believe it would occur to her to send any special word to Fräulein."

"She might be put under suspicion if she addressed a letter to any one with a German name even if she lived in the United States."

"No one but Ethel Blue has had a letter from Mademoiselle since, she left," said Helen. "We should have heard of it, I'm sure."

"Well, what do you say to the plan? Can't we send a cable signed by the 'Secretary of the United Service Club'?"

"I think it would be a good use to put the Club money to," approved James, the treasurer.

"If you say so I'll send it when I get back to New York this afternoon. How shall we word it?"

"Mademoiselle Justine Millerand, Care Monsieur Millerand, Minister of War, Bordeaux, France," said Roger, slowly.

"Cut out 'Mademoiselle' and 'Monsieur,'" suggested Margaret. "We must remember that our remarks cost about a quarter a word in times of peace and war prices may be higher."

"Cut out 'of War,'" said Ethel Brown.

"There's only one 'Bordeaux,'" added Margaret.

"A dollar and a quarter saved already," said James thoughtfully. "Now let's have the message."

"What's the matter with Tom's original suggestion—'Is Schuler dead'?" asked Ethel Blue. "I suppose we must leave out the 'Mr.' if we are going to be economical."

"Sign it 'Morton, Secretary United Service Club, Rosemont.' I'll file Ethel Blue's address—at the cable office so the answer will be sent to her if one comes."

Ethel Blue looked somewhat agitated at the prospect of receiving a cable almost from the battlefield, but she said nothing.

"The United Service Club was the last group of people she saw in America, you see," Tom went on, "so Edward thinks she'll know at once whom the message comes from and she'll guess that the high school scholars want to know about their former teacher."

"I have a feeling in my bones that she'll get the message and that she'll answer," said Ethel Blue.

"If she doesn't get it we shan't have done any harm," mused Ethel Brown, "and if she does get it and answers then we shall have done a lot of good by getting the information for Fräulein."

"We needn't tell anybody about it outside of our families and then there won't be any expectations to be disappointed."

"It certainly would be best not to tell Fräulein."

"That's settled, then," said Tom, "and I'll send the message the moment I reach town this afternoon."

"It's the most thrilling thing I ever had anything to do with," Ethel Blue whispered.

CHAPTER XIX

LEATHER AND BRASS

THE following week was filled with expectation of a reply from Mademoiselle, but none came though every ring at the Mortons' doorbell was answered with the utmost promptness by one or another of the children who made a point of rushing to the door before Mary could reach it.

"I suppose we could hardly expect to have a reply," sighed Ethel Blue, "but it would have been so splendiferous if it did come!"

Thanks to Dicky's escapade the last Saturday afternoon had been so broken in upon that the Club decided that they must have an all-day session on the next Saturday. Roger had promised to teach the others how to do the leather and brass work in which he had become quite expert, and he was talking to himself about it as he was dressing after doing his morning work.

"This business of working in leather for orphan children makes a noise like toil to me," he soliloquized. "But think of the joy of the kids when they receive a leather penwiper, though they aren't yet old enough to write, or a purse when they haven't any shekels to put into it!"

"Ro—ger," came a voice from a long way off.

"Let's go over to Dorothy's now," Roger called back as if it had been Ethel Brown who was late.

"I should say so! The Watkinses and Hancocks said they'd be there at ten and it must be that now. I'll call Ethel Blue and Helen," and Ethel Brown's voice came from a greater distance than before.

The other girls were not to be discovered, however, and when Roger and Ethel arrived at Dorothy's they found all the rest waiting for them.

"Roger cut a slip ten inches long and four inches wide" "Roger cut a slip ten inches long and four inches wide"

Corner for Blotter Pad Corner for Blotter Pad

"Where's this professor of leather?" called Tom as he heard Roger's steps on the attic stairs.

"And brass," added Roger grandly as he appeared in the doorway.

"No one disputes the brass," returned Tom, and Roger roared cheerfully and called out "Bull's-eye!"

"Now, then," began Roger seating himself at the head of the table, "with apologies to the president I'll call this solemn meeting to order—that is, as much order as there can be with Dicky around."

Dicky was even then engaged in trying to make a hole in Ethel Blue's shoe with a leather punch, but he was promptly suppressed and placed between the Ethels before his purpose was accomplished.

"You've got him interned there," remarked James, using a phrase that was becoming customary in the newspaper accounts of the care of prisoners.

"I'm going to start you people making corners for a big blotting pad," said Roger, "not because the orphans will want a blotting pad, but because they are easy to make and you can adapt the idea to lots of other articles."

"Fire ahead," commanded James.

"You make a paper pattern to fit your corner—so fashion," and Roger tore a sheet of paper off a pad and cut a slip ten inches long and four inches wide. A point in the middle of the long side he placed on the corner of the big blotter that lay before him and then he folded the rest of the paper around the corner. The result was a smooth triangle on the face of the blotter and a triangle at the back just like it except that it was split up the middle.

"Here's your pattern," said Roger slipping it off. "When you make this of brass or copper it's a good plan to round these back corners so there won't be any sharp points to stick into you or to scratch the desk."

"The orphans' mahogany."

"Or Grandfather Emerson's. I'm going to inflict a set on him at Christmas."

"I should think it would be hard to work on such dinky little things," remarked James who had large hands.

"You don't cut them out of your big sheet of copper or your big piece of leather yet. You draw the size of this small pattern on to a larger piece of paper and you draw your ornamental design right where you want it on the face of the triangle—so."

"More work for Ethel Blue, making original designs."

"She might get up some U. S. C. designs and have them copyrighted," suggested Helen.

"Until she does we'll have to use these simple figures that I traced out of a book the other day."

"Why couldn't we use our stenciling designs?"

"You could, if they are the right size. That star pattern you put oh a doll's skirt would be just the ticket—just one star for each corner."

"We might put U. S. C. in each corner."

"Or U. in one corner and S. in another, and C. in a third and a star or something in the fourth."

"Or the initials of the person you give it to."

"We've got the size of the corner piece as it is when it's unfolded and with its design on it, all drawn on this piece of paper. Now you tack your sheet of brass on to a block of wood and lay a sheet of carbon paper over it and your design on that and trace ahead."

"I see, I see," commented Margaret. "When you take it off, there you have the size of your corner indicated and the star or whatever you're going to ornament it with, all drawn in the right place."

"Exactly. Now we tackle the brass itself."

"It seems to me we ought to have some tools for that."

"A light hammer and a wire nail—that's all. See the point of this nail? It has been filed flat and rather dull. I made enough for everybody to have one—not you, sir," and he snatched away one of them from Dicky just as that young man was about to nail Ethel Brown's dress on to the edge of her chair.

"Dicky will have to be interned at home if he isn't quiet." The president shook her head at the honorary member.

"First you go around the whole outline, tapping the nail gently, stroke by stroke, until the line of the design is completely hammered in."

"That isn't hard," said Tom. "Watch me."

"When the outline is made you take another wire nail that has been filed perfectly flat on the bottom and go over the whole background with it."

"I see, I see," cried Ethel Blue. "That makes the design stand out puffily and smooth against a sort of motheaten background."

"For eloquent description commend me to Ethel Blue," declared Margaret.

"She's right, though. You can make the moth holes of different size by using nails of different sizes. There are regular tools that come, too, with different pounding surfaces so it's possible to make quite a variety of backgrounds."

"This mothy one is pretty enough for me," declared Margaret.

"I don't much like that name for it, but it is pretty, just the same," insisted Roger. "When you've hammered down the background you take out the tacks and cut out your whole corner with this pair of shears that is made to cut metal. Then you fold over the backs just the way you folded over the paper to find the shape originally."

"It's not so terribly easy to bend," commented Ethel Blue.

"Shape them along the edge of your block of wood. Persuade them down— so, and fold them back—so. Tap them into place with your wooden mallet. There you are."

The finished corner was passed from hand to hand and duly admired.

"Rub it shiny with any brass polish, if you like it bright," directed Roger.

"It's fashionable for coppers to be dull now," said Helen.

"You ladies know more about fashions of all sorts than I should ever pretend to," said her brother meekly. "I like metals to shine, myself."

"What are some of the articles we can start in to make now that we know how?" questioned Margaret.

"All sorts of things for the desk—a paper knife and a roller blotter and a case to hold the inkwell and a clip to keep papers from blowing away. The work is just the same, no matter what you're making. It's all a matter of getting the outlines of different objects and then bending them up carefully after you've hammered the design and got them cut out well."

"Why can't you make all sorts of boxes?" asked James whose mind had run to boxes ever since his week of work upon them.

"You can. All sorts and sizes. Line them with silk or leather. Leather wears best."

"How far is the leather work like the metal work?" asked Ethel Brown. "It seemed to be the same as far as the point where you tacked them on to the wooden block."

"A beauty leather mat" "A beauty leather mat"

"It is the same except that you wet the leather before you tack it on to the block. When you put your design on to the leather you don't need to use carbon paper. Borrow one of Ethel Brown's knitting needles and run it over the design that you have drawn on the paper placed over the leather, and it will leave a tiny groove on the damp leather."

"That's a simple instrument."

"A three cornered purse that doesn't need any sewing" "A three cornered purse that doesn't need any sewing"

"The steel tooler you take next is simple, too. You deepen the groove with its edge and then take the flat part of the tooler and go over every bit of the leather outside of the design, pressing it and polishing it with great care."

"I suppose that gives the leather a different texture."

The three cornered purse completed The three cornered purse completed

"It seems to. It makes the design show more, anyway."

"I saw a beauty leather mat the other day with a cotton boll design that puffed right up from the background.

"The cotton boll caught our little Dorothy's eye, of course! You make your design puff out by rubbing it on the back with a round headed tool. Your mat probably had the puffed up part filled with wax so it wouldn't smash down again when something heavy was placed on it."

"I think it did; it felt hard."

"If you do puff out any part of your pattern you have to tool over the design again, because the outline will have lost its sharpness."

"The mat I saw was colored."

"That's easy. There are colors that come especially for using on leather. You float them on when the leather is wet and you can get beautiful effects."

"You ought not to cut out your leather corners until they are dry, I suppose?"

"They ought to be thoroughly dry. If you want a lining for a purse or a cardcase you can paste in either silk or a thin leather. It's pretty to make an openwork design and let the lining show through."

"How about sewing purses? It must be hard work."

"Helen does mine on the machine. She says it isn't much trouble if she goes slowly and takes a few stitches back at the ends so they won't come apart. But I'm going to show you how to make a little three cornered purse that doesn't need any sewing—only two glove snappers."

So simple was this pattern that each of them had finished one by the time that Grandmother Emerson's car came to take them all over to luncheon at her house.

CHAPTER XX

THE ETHELS COOK TO KEEP

ANOTHER week rolled on and still no reply came to the cable that the Club had sent to Mademoiselle Millerand.

"Either she hasn't received it," said Ethel Blue, who felt a personal interest because it had been signed by her as Secretary of the club, "or Mr. Schuler is dead and she doesn't want to tell us."

"It's pretty sure to be one or the other," said Ethel Brown. "I suppose we might as well forget that we tried to do anything about it."

"Have you heard Roger or Helen say anything about Fräulein lately?"

"Helen said she looked awfully sad and that she was wearing black. Evidently she has no hope."

"Poor Fräulein!"

Bag for a doll, a child or a grown-up Bag for a doll, a child or a grown-up

"What are we going to do this week?"

"I've planned the cunningest little travelling bag for a doll. It's a straight strip of leather, tooled in a pretty pattern. It's doubled in halves and there is a three-cornered piece let in at the ends to give a bit more room."

"How do you fasten it?"

"Like a Boston bag, with a strap that goes over the top."

"You could run a cord in and out parallel with the top and pull it up."

"I believe I'll make two and try both ways."

"You could make the same pattern only a little larger for a wrist bag for an older child."

"And larger still for a shopping bag for a grown person."

"That's as useful a pattern as Helen's and Margaret's wrapper pattern! Do you realize that this is the week that we ought to cook?"

"Is it? We'll have to hurry fearfully! Are you perfectly sure the things will keep?"

"I've talked it over several times with Miss Dawson, the domestic science teacher. She has given me some splendid receipts and some information about packing. She says there won't be any doubt of their travelling all right."

"We'll have to cook every afternoon, then. We'd better go over the receipts and see if we have all the materials we need."

"We know about the cookies and the fruit cake and the fudge. We've made all those such a short time ago that we know we have those materials. Here are ginger snaps," she went on, examining her cook book. "We haven't enough molasses I'm sure, and I'm doubtful about the ginger."

"Let me see."

Ethel Blue read over the receipt.

" pt. molasses—dark

cup butter

tablespoon ginger

teaspoon soda

teaspoon cinnamon

"About quarts flour, or enough more to make a thick dough.

"Sift flour, soda, and spices together. Melt the butter, put the molasses in a big bowl, add the butter, then the flour gradually, using a knife to cut it in. When stiff enough to roll, roll out portions quite thin on a floured board, cut out with a cookie cutter or with the cover of a baking powder can. Place them on greased tins, leaving a little space between each cookie. Bake in a hot oven about five minutes."

"Miss Dawson says we must let the cookies get perfectly cold before we pack them. Then we must wrap them in paraffin paper and pack them tightly into a box."

"They ought to be so tight that they won't rattle round and break."

"If we could get enough tin boxes it would be great."

"Let's ask Grandmother Emerson and Aunt Louise and all Mother's friends to save their biscuit boxes for us."

"We ought to have thought of asking them before. And we must go out foraging for baking powder tins to steam the little fruit puddings and the small loaves of Boston brown bread in."

"What a jolly idea!"

"Miss Dawson says that when they are cold we can slip them out of their tins and brush the bread and pudding and cake over with pure alcohol. That will kill the mould germs and it will all be evaporated by the time they are opened."

"If there is paraffin paper around them, too, and they are slipped back into their little round tins it seems to me they ought to be as cosy and good as possible."

"I'm awfully taken with the individual puddings. We can make them all different sizes according to the size of the tins we get hold of. Doesn't this sound good?"

Ethel read aloud the pudding receipt with an appreciative smile.

"Steamed Fruit Pudding

"½ cups flour

teaspoons baking powder

½ teaspoon salt

¼ teaspoon cinnamon

½ teaspoon nutmeg or ginger

cup chopped suet

cup chopped raisins

½ cup cleaned currants

cup water or milk

cup molasses (dark)

"Sift soda, salt, baking powder, and spice with the flour, add the suet and fruit, then the molasses and milk. Mix well. Fill moulds two-thirds full. Steam three hours."

"When we do them up we can arrange them so that no bundle will contain both a fruit cake and a fruit pudding. We must have variety."

"I asked particularly about wheat bread. The papers say that that is scarce, you know."

"Did Miss Dawson say it would travel?"

"No, she thought it would be as hard as shoe leather. But she says the Boston brown bread ought to be soft enough even after six weeks. If we can make enough small loaves—"

"Baking powder tin loaves—"

"Yes—to have a loaf of bread and a fruit cake or a fruit pudding or a box of cookies—"

"That is, one cake—"

"—and some candy in each package that we do up it will give variety."

"It sounds good to me. We'll have to hide all our things away from Roger."

"Listen to this receipt:

"Boston Brown Bread

" cup rye meal (or flour)

cup granulated corn-meal

cup Graham flour

cups sour milk or ¾ cups sweet milk or water

teaspoon salt

¾ teaspoon soda

¾ cup molasses (dark)

"Mix and sift the dry ingredients, add molasses and milk, stir until well mixed, turn into a well greased mould, steam ½ hours. The cover should be greased before being placed on the mould, then tied down with a string, otherwise the bread might force off the cover. The mould should never be filled more than two-thirds full. For steaming, place the mould on a stand (or on nails laid flat) in a kettle of boiling water, allowing water to come half way up around mould, cover closely, and steam, add, as needed, more boiling water."

"'Mould' is polite for baking powder tin."

"I wish our family was small enough for us to have them. They're just too dear!"

"Some time after the Christmas Ship sails let's make some for the family—one for each person."

"That's a glorious idea. I never do have enough on Sunday morning and you know how Roger teases every one of us to give him part of ours."

"All these 'eats' that travel so well will be splendid to send for Christmas gifts to people at a distance, won't they? People like Katharine Jackson in Buffalo."

"And the Wilson children at Fort Myer," and the Ethels named other young people whom they had met at different garrisons and Navy Yards.

"Here are three kinds of candies that Miss Dawson says ought to travel perfectly if they're packed so they won't shake about Here's 'Roly Poly' to start with. I can see Katharine's eyes shining over that."

"And the orphans', too."

Ethel read the receipt.

"Roly Poly

" lbs. brown sugar

cup cream

tablespoons butter

½ pint (cup) chopped figs

cup chopped almonds

cups chopped dates

cup citron, cut in pieces

½ cup chopped pecans

½ cup chopped cherries

½ cup chopped raisins

"Cook sugar, cream and butter together until a little forms a soft ball when dropped in a cup of cold water. Then add the nuts and fruit. Put it all in a wet cotton bag, mould into a roll on a smooth surface. Remove from the bag and cut as desired."

"I like the sound of 'Sea Foam.' Della tried that, and said it was delicious.

"Sea Foam

" cups brown sugar

½ cup water

teaspoon vanilla

cup chopped nuts

white of egg

"Beat the white of egg until stiff. Boil the sugar and water together until a little forms a soft ball when dropped in a cup of cold water. Add the vanilla and nuts, beat this into the white of egg. When it stiffens pour it into a greased pan, or drop it by spoonsful on the pan."

"It sounds delicious. When we fill James's pretty boxes with these goodies and tie them with attractive paper and cord they are going to look like 'some' Christmas to these poor little kiddies."

"Don't you wish we could see them open them?"

"If Mademoiselle would only send that Belgian baby we really could."

"I'm afraid Mademoiselle has forgotten us utterly."

"It isn't surprising. But I wish she hadn't."

"We must get plenty of brown sugar. This 'Panocha' calls for it, as well as the 'Sea Foam' and the 'Roly Poly.'"

"We'll have to borrow a corner of Mary's storeroom for once."

"She won't mind. She's as interested as we are in the orphans. Let me see how the 'Panocha' goes.

"Panocha

" cups brown sugar

tablespoons butter

½ cup milk

½ cup chopped nuts of any kind.

"Boil sugar, butter, and milk together until a little forms a soft ball when dropped in a cup of cold water. Add the nuts, stir a few moments till slightly thick, drop by spoonsful on greased tins, or pour it into a greased tin. When cool cut in blocks."

The time given by the Ethels to preparing for their cooking operations was well spent. Never once did they have to call on Mary for something they had forgotten to order, and each afternoon was pronounced a success when it was over and its results lay before them.

"If we just had energy enough we might follow the plan that the candy store people do when they have a new clerk. They say that they let her eat all she wants to for the first few days and then she doesn't want any more. It would be fun to give the family all they wanted."

"We really ought to do it before we set the Club to work packing all these goodies, but I don't see how we can with those three boys. We never could fill them up so they'd stop eating."

"Nev-er!"

"Not Roger!"

"We'll just have to give them a lecture on self-control and set them to work."

"It's a glorious lot we've got. Where's Mother? We must show them to her and Grandmother and Aunt Louise."

So there was an exhibit of "food products" that brought the Ethels many compliments. Shelf upon shelf of their private kitchen was filled with boxes and tins, and every day added to the quantity, for Mary came in occasionally to bring a wee fruit cake, Aunt Louise sent over cookies, and Mrs. Emerson added a box of professional candy to the pile.

"They tell me at the candy store that very hard candy doesn't last well," she said. "It grows moist."

"That's why Miss Dawson gave me these receipts for softish candies like fudge. It's well to remember that at Christmas time when you're selecting candies for presents."

"I don't believe the Ethels ever will buy any candies again," said Mrs. Morton. "They've become so expert in making them that they quite look down on the professionals."

"Did you see the paper this morning?" asked Mrs. Emerson.

When the girls said that they had not, she produced a clipping.

"Grandfather thought that perhaps this might have escaped your notice, so he sent it over."

Ethel Brown took it and Ethel Blue read it over her shoulder.

CARGO FOR CHRISTMAS SHIP GATHERING HERE FROM EVERY STATE

Hundreds of cases containing every conceivable kind of gift for a child have been received at the Bush Terminal in Brooklyn, where the Christmas Ship Jason, which will carry the gifts of American children to the orphans of the European War is being loaded.

It became apparent that if the Jason were to get off within reasonable time, a tremendous force of sorters and packers would have to be employed. When the situation was presented over the telephone to Secretary of the Navy Daniels he secured authorization for Gen. Wood to assign sixty soldiers to help to get the cargo ready. These men appeared for duty yesterday afternoon.

Secretary Daniels has assigned Lieut.-Commander Courtney to command the Christmas Ship.

"What a fine Santa Claus-y feeling Commander Courtney must have," said Mrs. Morton. "He's a friend of your father's, Ethel Brown."

"Think of being Santa Claus to all Europe!"

"Our parcels won't be very visible among several millions, will they?"

"You have a wonderfully creditable collection for ten youngsters working so short a time."

"Mr. Watkins is keeping in touch with the ship so that we can make use of every day that she's delayed. Tom telephoned to Roger this afternoon that he had been over to the Bush Terminal and they were sure they wouldn't start before the th of November.

"That gives us almost a week more, you see."

"Do you think we could go to New York to see the Jason sail?" asked Ethel Blue and both girls waited eagerly for the reply.

"Aunt Louise and I were saying that the Club ought to go in a body."

"If only she doesn't sail during school hours."

"Even then I think we might manage it for once," smiled Mrs. Morton, and the Ethels rushed off to tell Roger and Helen the plan and to telephone it to Margaret and James.

CHAPTER XXI

THE CHRISTMAS SHIP SAILS

THE Rosemont and Glen Point members of the U. S. C. did not wait for the Watkinses to join them on Saturday before beginning to do up the parcels for the Santa Claus Ship. All the small bundles were wrapped and tied in Dorothy's attic, but after Mrs. Smith had made a careful examination of the attic stairs she came to the conclusion that the large packing cases into which they must be put for transportation to the Bush Terminal in Brooklyn could not be taken down without damage to the walls. It was therefore decided that when the bundles were ready they were to be brought downstairs and there packed into several large cases which had been donated for the purpose by the local dry goods dealer and the shoe store man.

Each of these huge boxes James declared to be probably as large as the mysterious house which Roger was going to propose for some sort of club work in the spring. They had been delivered early in the week and were established on the porch at the back of the Smith cottage awaiting the contents that were to bring pleasure to hundreds of expectant children.

Doctor Hancock was so busy that he could not bring Margaret's and James's collection to Rosemont when it was wanted there, so Mrs. Emerson went to Glen Point in her car and brought it back filled high with the result of James's pasting. It was necessary to have all his boxes to pack the candies and cookies and small gifts in.

Every afternoon a busy throng gathered in the attic, wrapping and tying and labelling the work that kept them all so busy for the previous two months.

"We must do up every package just as carefully as if we were going to put it on our own Christmas tree," Helen decided. "I think half the fun of Christmas is untying the bundles and having the room all heaped up with tissue paper and bright ribbons."

The Club had laid in a goodly store of tissue paper of a great variety of colors, buying it at wholesale and thus obtaining a discount over the retail price. The question of what to tie with was a subject of discussion.

"We certainly can't afford ribbon," Ethel Brown declared. "Even the narrowest kind is too expensive when we have to have hundreds of yards of it."

"We ought to have thought about it before," said Helen looking rather worried, as this necessity should have been foreseen by the president. "I'll go right over to town and get something now," she added, putting on her hat. "Have any of you girls any ideas on the subject?"

"I have," replied Dorothy. "You know that bright colored binding that dressmakers use on seams? It's sometimes silk and sometimes silk and—"

"Cotton? Ha!"

"Silk and cotton; yes, ma'am. It comes in all colors and it's just the right width and it costs a good deal less than real ribbon."

"I suppose we can get the rolls by wholesale in assorted colors, can't we?"

"I should suppose so."

"I have an idea, too," offered Margaret who had come over on the trolley after school was over. "There's a tinsel cord, silver and gilt, that doesn't cost much and it looks bright and pretty. It would be just the thing."

"I've seen that. It does look pretty. For home packages you can stick a sprig of holly or a poinsettia in the knot and it makes it C-H-A-R-M-I-N-G," spelled Ethel Blue, giving herself a whirl in her excitement.

"But we can't use stick-ups on our Christmas Ship parcels, you know."

"That's so, but the tinsel string just by itself is quite pretty enough."

"I'll bring back bushels," said Helen. "You have enough to go on with for a while."

"One year when Mother and I were caught at the last minute on Christmas Eve without any ribbon," said Dorothy, "—it was after the shops had closed, I remember, we found several bundles that we had overlooked—we tied them with ordinary red and green string twisted together. It looked holly-fied."

"That would be easy to do," said Roger. "See, put two balls of twine, one red and one green in a box and punch a hole in the top and let the two colors come out of the hole. Then use them just as if they were one cord. See?"

"As he talked he manufactured a twine box, popping into it not only the red and green balls about which he had been talking, but, on the other side of a slip of pasteboard which he put in for a partition, a ball of pink and a ball of blue.

"Watch Roger developing another color scheme," cried Ethel Blue. "I'm going to follow that out," and she proceeded to make up a collection of parcels wrapped in pink tissue paper tied with blue string, in blue paper tied with pink cord and in white tied with Roger's combination.

"There's one family fitted out with a lot of presents all naturally belonging together," she cried.

"I rather like that notion myself," announced James gravely, adjusting his lame leg to a more comfortable position. "Please hand me that brown and yellow tissue, somebody. I'm going to make a lot of bundles along the color lines that my auburn haired sister uses in her dress."

"Observant little Jimmy," commented Margaret.

"Here you perceive, ladies, that I am doing up the bundles with brown and yellow and burnt orange and tango, and lemon color, and I'm tying them with a contrast—brown with orange and buttercup yellow with brown and lemon yellow with white and so on. Good looking, eh?" he finished, pointing with pride to his group of attractive parcels.

"I'm going to do a bunch with a mixture of all sorts," announced Roger. "Here's a green tied with red and a white tied with green and a pink tied with white and a brown tied with tango, and violet tied with blue, und so weiter, as our Fräulein says when she means 'and so forth' and can't remember her English fast enough."

"Poor Fräulein! It will be a hard Christmas for her."

"She brought in the last of her work and Mrs. Hindenburg's yesterday. Such a mound of knitting!"

"Has any one been to the Old Ladies' Home to gather up what they have there?" asked James.

"Roger went early this morning before school. Perhaps those old ladies haven't been busy! See that pile?"

"All theirs? Good work," and James set about tying up the soft and comfortable knitted mufflers and wristlets and socks, first in tissue paper with a ribbon or a bright cord and then with a stouter wrapper of ordinary paper. He marked on each package what was in it.

"If the people who are doing the sorting and repacking at the Bush Terminal can know what is in each bundle it is going to help them a lot," remarked methodical James.

The packing of the candies and cookies took especial care, for they had to be wrapped in paraffin paper and tightly wedged in the fancy boxes awaiting them before they could be wrapped with their gay outside coverings.

"We want them to arrive with some shape still left to them and not merely a boxful of crumbs," said Ethel Brown earnestly.

Except for the collections of varied presents which they had made for the sake of the color schemes of their wrappings—an arrangement with which Helen was much pleased when she came back laden with ribbons and cord—the gifts were packed according to their kind. Every article of clothing was wrapped separately and the bundles were labelled, each with the name of the article within, and then put into one large box. It was only by great squeezing that the knitted articles were persuaded to go into the same case.

In another box were the candies and cookies and cakes and breads. The grocer from whom they had bought the materials for their cooking had contributed a dozen tins of peaches.

In still another case went the seemingly innumerable small parcels that held toys or little gifts. Here were the metal pieces and the leather coin purses and the stuffed animals and the dolls. Doctor Hancock had sent over a box of raisins and Mrs. Watkins had sent out from town a box of figs and a few of these goodies with two or three pieces of candy, went into every article that could be made to serve as a container. Of this sort were the innumerable fancy bags made of silk bits and of cretonne and of scraps of velvet which the girls had put together when other work flagged. Many of the pretty little baskets held a pleasant amount of sweeties, and the tiny leather travelling bags and the larger wrist bags of tooled leather were lined with a piece of paraffin paper enclosing something for sweet-toothed European children.

James's boxes, with those made by the others, held out wonderfully.

"You certainly put in a good week's work with the paste pot," declared Roger admiringly as he filled the last one with sugar cookies and tied it with green and red twine to harmonize with its covering of holly paper.

The Watkinses had sent out their offerings, for they wanted what they had at home to be packed with the other Club articles, even though they lived nearer than the rest to the place from which the ship was going to steam. When this additional collection was prepared and packed it was found that there were three big packing cases.

"Good for the U. S. C.!" cried the boys as the last nail went into the last cover.

James, who printed well, painted the address neatly on the tops and sides, and they all watched with vivid interest the drayman who hauled them, away, generously contributing his services to the Christmas cause.

After all their hurry it seemed something of a hardship when they were informed that the sailing of the ship was delayed for several days because the force of packers, large as it was, could not prepare all the parcels in time for the tenth of the month.

"The paper says there are more than sixty car-loads of gifts," read Ethel Blue to her interested family, "and five or six million separate presents."

"No wonder they're delayed!"

Yet after all they were glad of the delay for the Jason finally sailed at noon of the fourteenth, and that was Saturday. The Hancocks went in to New York and over to Brooklyn in the Doctor's car and Mrs. Emerson's big touring car held all the Mortons and Dorothy and her mother, and Fräulein and her mother, though it was a tight squeeze.

"The old woman who lived in a shoe must have been on her way to a Christmas Ship," cried Grandmother when Roger tossed Dicky in "on top of the heap of Ethels," as he described it and took up his own station on the running board.

The pier at the Bush Terminal in Brooklyn was already well crowded with people and motors when the Rosemont party arrived. The Watkinses and the Hancocks were already there. Freight cars stood at one side, freight cars empty now of their loads of good cheer. Everybody was laughing and happy and in a Christmas mood, and the boy band from St. John's Home in Brooklyn made merry music.

Thanks to Mrs. Morton's acquaintance with Lieutenant-Commander Courtney, who was in command of the ship, she and her flock had been invited to hear the speeches of farewell made in the main saloon by representatives of the city of New York.

Roger led the way to the gang plank which stretched from the pier to the deck of the huge navy collier.

"Old Jason looks grim enough in his gray war paint," he commented.

"But those great latticed arms of the six cranes look as if he were trying to play Christmas tree," suggested Mrs. Emerson.

The speeches were full of good will and Christmas cheer. Back on to the pier went the listeners and then amid the cheers of the throng on the dock and the whistles of near-by boats and the strains of "The Star Spangled Banner" from the boys' band and the waving of handkerchiefs and hats, the huge gray steamer slipped out into the stream and started on her way across the ocean.

It was when the U. S. C. was making its way back to the automobiles that a piercing scream attracted their attention.

"That sounds like Fräulein's voice," said Helen, looking about for the source of the cry.

"Meine Tochter!" exclaimed Mrs. Hindenburg at the same moment.

And then they came upon Fräulein, her arms about the neck of a bearded man, who stroked her hair and cheek with one hand while with the other he clung to one of the crutches which gave him but an insecure support.

"Lieber Heinrich!" cried Mrs. Hindenburg as she caught sight of the tableau.

"It's—yes, I believe it's Mr. Schuler! Look, Helen, do you think it is?" whispered Roger.

"It must be," returned Helen. "It's hard to tell with that beard, but I'm almost sure it is."

"His leg! Oh, Helen, his leg is gone!" lamented Ethel Blue.

The Rosemont party's certainty was relieved by Mrs. Hindenburg who turned to them, beaming.

"It iss Mr. Schuler; it iss Heinrich," she explained. "He has lost his leg. What matter? He is here and the Tochter is happy!"

Happy indeed was Fräulein when she turned her tear-stained face toward the others.

"He has come," she said simply, while the rest crowded around and shook hands.

It seemed that he had obtained leave to return to America because he had lost his leg and could fight no more. Yes, he said, Mademoiselle Millerand had nursed him when his leg was taken off.

The spectators of the moving pictures looked at each other and nodded.

Mademoiselle had sent a message to the Secretary of the United Service Club, he went on. It was—he took a slip of paper from his pocket book.

"Message received. Answered in person."

The Club members laughed at this whose whole meaning it was clear that Mr. Schuler did not appreciate.

He had arrived, it seemed, only two hours before, on an Italian boat, and had heard on the way up from Quarantine of the sailing of the Christmas Ship and so had crossed to wave a farewell before going out to Rosemont.

"And here I have found my best fortune," he said over and over again, his eyes resting fondly on Fräulein's face.

CHAPTER XXII

A WEDDING AND A SURPRISE

IT was a simple wedding that the U. S. C. went to in a body a few days after the arrival of the convalescent German soldier. Mr. Wheeler, the principal of the high school, acted as best man, and Miss Dawson, the domestic science teacher, was maid of honor, but Fräulein also gathered about her in the cottage sitting-room where the ceremony took place a group of the young girls who had been kindest to her when she was in trouble.

"I want you and the Ethels and Dorothy," she said to Helen; "and if your friends, Della and Margaret, would come with you it would give me greatest pleasure."

So the girls, all dressed in white, and wearing the forget-me-not pins that Grandfather Emerson insisted on giving them for the occasion, clustered around the young teacher, and the three boys, a forget-me-not in each scarfpin, held the ribbons that pressed gently back the cordial friends who were happy in Fräulein's happiness.

It was the Club that decorated the house with brown sedges and stalks of upstanding tawny corn and vines of bittersweet. And it was the Club that sang a soft German marriage song as the bride and groom drove off toward the setting sun in Grandmother Emerson's car.

Life seemed rather flat to the members of the U. S. C. after the wedding. For the last two months they had been so busy that every hour had been filled with work and play-work, and now that there was nothing especial scheduled for every waking moment it seemed as if they had nothing at all to do.

"We'll have to ask Roger about his house," laughed James who came over with Margaret one afternoon and confessed to the same feeling.

"Not yet," answered Helen.

"Helen is full of ideas up to her very eyebrows, I believe," said Ethel Blue. "She's just giving us a holiday."

"Mother said we needed one," assented Helen. "After we've had a few days' rest we can start on something else. There's no need to call on Roger yet awhile."

"Why not? My idea is a perfectly good one," insisted Roger, strolling in.

Just at this minute Mary entered with a note for "The Secretary of the United Service Club."

"For you, Ethel Blue," said Roger, handing it to his cousin.

Ethel Blue slipped a cutter under the edge while the others waited expectantly, for the address indicated that the contents was of interest to all of them.

"What does this mean?" she cried as she read. "What is it? Is it true?"

She was so excited that they all crowded around her to see what had taken away her power of explanation.

The letter was signed "Justine Millerand."

"Mademoiselle," cried all who could see the signature.

"She says," read Ethel Blue, finding her strength again, "'Here is the Belgian baby you asked for. She is two years old and her name is "Elisabeth," after the Queen of Belgium!'"

"Is that all?"

"That's all."

"But she says, 'Here is the Belgian baby.' Where is the Belgian baby?"

They turned toward Mary who had remained in the room.

"There's a Red Cross nurse in the reception room," she explained. "She said she'd rather you read the letter first."

They made a rush for the door. Roger reached it first and ushered the nurse into the living room. She was dressed in her grey uniform and sheltered under her cape the thinnest, wannest mite of humanity that ever the Club had seen outside of the streets of a city slum.

"Mademoiselle Millerand said you had asked for a Belgian baby," she began, but she was interrupted by a cry from the entire throng.

"We did; we did," they exclaimed so earnestly that any doubts she may have felt about the cordiality of their reception of her nursling were banished at once.

"Your mother?" she asked.

"I don't believe Mother really expected it to come, any more than we did," replied Helen frankly, "but she will love it just as we will, and we'll take the very best of care of her."

She offered her finger to Elisabeth, who clutched it and gazed solemnly at her out of her sunken blue eyes.

Ethel Blue in the back of the group gave a sob.

"She'll pick up soon when she has good food every day," the nurse reassured them, and then she told them of her own experiences.

She had been, it seemed, in the same hospital with Mademoiselle in Belgium. Out on the field one day a bit of shrapnel had wounded her foot so that she was forced to come home. Mademoiselle had asked her to bring over this mite "to the kindest young people in the world," and here she was.

The baby's father and mother were both dead, she went on. That she knew.

"Are you sure her name is Elisabeth?" asked Dorothy.

"That's what she calls herself."

By this time Elisabeth had made friends with every one of them and was sitting comfortably on one of Roger's knees while Dicky occupied the other and made acceptable gestures toward her.

"She'll be happy here," said the nurse, and rose to explain her visit to Mrs. Morton.

Like the girls, Mrs. Morton had not expected that Mademoiselle would respond to their request for a Belgian baby and she was somewhat taken back by its appearance.

"I can see that you did not look for her," the nurse suggested, "but when you are on the spot and are seeing such hideous distress every day and a chance opens to relieve just one little child, it is more than you can resist. I know that is why Mademoiselle Millerand sent her."

"I quite understand," responded Mrs. Morton cordially. "Elisabeth shall have a happy home in Rosemont."

"And a baker's dozen of fathers and mothers to make up for her own," said James.

"And we're grateful to you for bringing her," said Ethel Blue, offering her hand.

It was after the nurse had had a cup of tea and had returned to New York that Helen called the Club to order formally.

"The Club has got its work cut out for it for a long time to come," she said. "I don't think we have any right to bring this baby over to America and then send it to an orphanage, though that would be the easiest way to do."

"We'll never do that," said Margaret firmly.

"If we are going to take care of it it means that we'll have to earn money for it and give it our personal care. Now, all in favor of accepting Elisabeth as our Club baby, say 'Aye.'"

There was a hearty assent.

"There are no contrary-minded," declared the president. "From now on she belongs to us."

"And here's my forget-me-not pin to prove it," said Ethel Blue, fastening it on the baby's dress.

"Just what we'll have to do about her we must think out carefully and talk over with our mothers," went on Helen. "But this minute we can accept our new club member and cry all together, 'Three cheers for Elisabeth of Belgium.'"

And at the shout that followed, Elisabeth of Belgium gave her first faint smile.

THE END

www.ingramcontent.com/pod-product-compliance
Lightning Source LLC
Chambersburg PA
CBHW080908190726
48294CB00008B/2008